Deep Secrets
Also by P.K. Norton

If you love reading solid mysteries with a heroine you can identify with, then look no further than novelist P.K. Norton. Deep Secrets *is her latest installment featuring intrepid insurance investigator Amy Lynch. Amy is no ordinary sleuth and the mystery set in and around Cape Cod will keep you guessing to the end!*

~Jordan Rich, WBZ iHeart Radio

"Norton draws on her experience working in the insurance industry to good effect in this latest series outing ... (she) manages to make insurance-related details as compelling as evidence collection in a conventional murder mystery. The plot is well-paced... the characters well-drawn. An entertaining, well-plotted mystery that offers good characterization and unexpected twists and turns."

~Kirkus Reviews

Dead Drop
Also by P.K. Norton

Does the past ever really leave us? Not in Amy Lynch's world. What starts out to be a well-deserved vacation for Amy – volunteering at an archaeological dig on the outskirts of Paris – turns ugly when the head archaeologist is found dead at the dig-site. A recently uncovered relic from World War II threatens to expose treachery and betrayal from the time of the German Occupation. It endangers the life of anybody bold enough to delve into its significance.

New England Casualty and Indemnity, the insurance company where Amy works as a claims investigator, is insuring the dig. Amy's world turns upside-down as she reverts from vacation mode to conduct a full-blown investigation. She meets with obstacles, resistance and threats to her own safety – as well as an adorable French detective – in her quest to unmask a traitor.

"Norton has created an engaging protagonist in Amy, who is bright, brave and tenacious. The tale features a small cast of characters, as many players disappear shortly after being introduced, so Amy has to carry the narrative load. Fortunately, she's up to the challenge; readers should quickly get involved in what happens to the feisty, heady heroine. With a neat twist in her fast-paced narrative, the author illustrates how events from 80 years in the past can affect people in the present, even Amy herself. Norton seamlessly blends history and mystery into a spellbinding thriller. This sequel accomplishes the unlikely feat of making an insurance investigator enthralling."

~Kirkus Reviews

Sweet Dreams, Sweet Death
Also by P.K. Norton

Everybody loves Chef Garcia's key lime coconut petit fours. Some even say they're to die for. When four guests die at a wedding at the Beaux Rêves Hotel, the famous petit fours are blamed.

Insurance investigator Amy Lynch flies to Key West to prepare for a wrongful death suit. Her investigation is beset with problems. Hotel management pushes for a quick settlement regardless of fault. Local police call it a tragic accident. Potential witnesses are missing, deceased, or unhelpful. Amy fends off pressures from all sides and encounters death everywhere. The health inspector dies in an accident; the local reporter turns up drowned; a homeless woman Amy befriends is found dead. And deceased wildlife crosses her path more than once.

As she forges on in the face of these obstacles, Amy wonders if Key West is the tropical paradise of the travel brochures or a petri dish of death.

"Norton weaves realistic professional procedure and unexpected emotional jolts into the otherwise erotic flavor of Key West, creating a debut that will seriously contend for all the "Best First" awards."

~Author Jeremiah Healy

"An impressively crafted and unfailingly entertaining novel by a master of the genre, Sweet Dreams, Sweet Death by P.K. Norton is the first volume in what promises to be a simply outstanding new series starring Amy Lynch, female investigator."

~James A. Cox
Editor-in-Chief, Midwest Book Review

DIRECT ELIMINATION

AN AMY LYNCH INVESTIGATION

P.K. NORTON

Visit our website at www.StillwaterPress.com for more information.

First Stillwater River Publications Edition

ISBN-13: 978-1-950-33993-8

1 2 3 4 5 6 7 8 9

Written by P.K. Norton
Cover design by Emma St. Jean
Published by Stillwater River Publications, Pawtucket, RI, USA.

Publisher's Cataloging-In-Publication Data
(Prepared by The Donohue Group, Inc.)

Names: Norton, P. K., author.
Title: Direct elimination / P.K. Norton.
Description: First Stillwater River Publications edition. | Pawtucket, RI, USA :
    Stillwater River Publications, [2020] | Series: An Amy Lynch
    investigation
Identifiers: ISBN 9781950339938 | ISBN 1950339939
Subjects: LCSH: Women insurance investigators--Massachusetts--Fiction. | Fire
    investigation--Massachusetts--Fiction. | LCGFT: Detective and mystery
    fiction.
Classification: LCC PS3614.O78266 D57 2020 | DDC 813/.6--dc23

DEDICATION

For Jack, my inspiration for this story – and my favorite fencer

ACKNOWLEDGEMENTS

With thanks to Jane and Lindsy for their editing skills, to Taro and Lisa for their advice on the finer points of fencing, to the Boston Fencing Club for allowing me to move their club to Dorchester and, as always, to Jack, who helped me bring Amy Lynch to Life.

CHAPTER 1

Two fire trucks screeched to a halt in front of the six-family dwelling at 12 Chadwick Street in the Dorchester section of Boston. A police car followed close behind. Flames were shooting out of the cellar and first-floor windows of the old wooden three-decker. Thick black smoke clouded the air. The blare of smoke alarms, combined with loud popping sounds, like fireworks, created a cacophony which competed with the sirens for attention, disturbing the peace of the chilly January afternoon, the first day of the new year.

A crowd of onlookers stepped aside as firefighters jumped from their vehicles. Some rushed to attach a hose to the nearby hydrant; others dashed up the front steps. The door was unlocked, but stuck less than half-way open. One of the men gave it a mighty kick and pushed with his heel. The door splintered and sagged. They finished demolishing the door, shoved the pieces aside, and ran inside the house – one of them to the cellar, two to the first floor apartments, one up the stairs.

The blaze was extinguished before it had a chance to spread beyond the left-hand apartment on the first floor. Once the hubbub quieted down, a voice bellowed from the cellar. "Get down here quick! You guys gotta see this."

As the men clomped down into the cellar, each in turn stopped short and stared. A young man dressed in white fencer's gear lay before them, épée in hand, the front of his jacket covered in blood.

CHAPTER 2

Sometimes New Year's resolutions simply refuse to be kept, and we are powerless in their wake. My plan for the coming year was to keep the paperwork and documentation associated with my job up-to-date and well-organized at all times. I had decided this with great reluctance. Investigating in the field was more interesting, and a lot more fun. Besides, the plaque on my desk identified me as Amy Lynch, Senior Claims Investigator at New England Casualty and Indemnity, not Senior Clerk. Nevertheless, I couldn't let the paperwork get away from me. Again.

Thus, I arrived at my office early on Monday, January 2, hoping to get caught up and organized, and make a clean start for the new year. Things were going fine for the first hour or so. I was encouraged by my progress, until …

"Good morning, Amy," a familiar voice beckoned from the doorway.

I looked up at my boyfriend Pete. The sight of him always made my lips smile and my heart flutter. After all, he was a bit of a hunk – tall and fair with killer green eyes. All dressed up in his three piece lawyer-going-to-court suit, he looked good, except perhaps for the sheepish expression on his face and the lack of the usual twinkle in his eyes. What was up with that?

"Hello to you." I said. "Please don't think I'm not thrilled to see you, but why aren't you in court?"

"I was. We settled at the last minute."

"And …?"

"My guy won."

I grinned at him. "Congratulations. Now you have the day free and you'd like to take me to brunch, or at least for coffee, right?" *And get me away from this damn paperwork.*

"We can do that if you want, but first I have something to tell you. It's not great news. I thought it'd be better to tell you in person. And sadly, this is business, not pleasure." He gave me a tight, forced smile.

"Your business or mine?"

The smile faded from his face. "Both, I'm afraid. My phone rang while I was in court this morning. It was my cousin, Andy Yesley. Calling about that six-family rental property in Dorchester he bought last November."

I wasn't sure I wanted to hear any more. "Do you mean the building the Underwriting Department didn't want to cover? The property that's only fifty percent occupied, not to mention in questionable condition? The property I used all my charms, as well as my pull as Senior Claims Investigator, to convince Underwriting to accept?" *And I never would have done any of that if I weren't so crazy about you.*

"Right. The building Andy is about to do a complete rehab on as soon as the weather improves and he comes up with more money."

I stood with my hands on my hips and stared at Pete. "I'm almost afraid to ask … but what happened?"

Pete studied his fingernails. "There was a fire yesterday."

Damn! The powers that be at New England Casualty and Indemnity tended to get really cranky when they agreed to write a

4

questionable risk as a favor to an employee and then it had a loss right away. "How bad is it?" I began pacing around my office.

"Andy says it's too early to tell. The blaze was extinguished fairly quickly. The firefighters' initial guess is that the damage is not extensive."

Spoken like a true lawyer. "But?"

"What makes you think there's a 'but'?"

I knew Pete too well to think otherwise. "Because you're here. So what is it? Was anybody hurt?" *And please tell me we're not dealing with a disaster.*

Pete avoided my eyes. "There was only one injury that I know of at this time."

"Go on." *How bad could it be?*

"They found a body in the cellar."

Double damn! I sank back into my chair. "What kind of a body?" *Perhaps a squirrel or a raccoon?*

"A young Canadian fellow. A fencer."

"OK, Pete. Sit down. Let's take this from the top."

Pete sat.

"First of all, please tell me why and how a Canadian fencer ended up dead in your cousin Andy's cellar." *And this better be good.*

Pete blew out a long, slow breath. "I've told you what Andy's like, Ames. He's a do-gooder, a bleeding heart liberal. He bought that property so he could provide decent, affordable housing to the working poor."

"The working poor Canadian fencers?"

"C'mon, Ames. Let me finish."

"Please do." I grabbed a pen and paper and prepared to make notes.

"You know the Boston Fencing Club's annual Hangover Open Tournament was yesterday."

"Of course I do. It's always on New Year's Day, hence the name."

"And we won't mention that I chose to forego competing in the tourney this year to spend time with you and your parents before they hit the road for Florida."

"And you know I love you for it. But please, continue with your story." The anticipation was making me seriously uncomfortable.

"So, Andy's good friend Freddie Dahlquist is the fencing coach at McGill University in Montréal. He wanted to bring his team down for the Open. His entire team of poor college students. They couldn't afford a hotel. Do-gooder Andy had a few vacant apartments. He offered to let the team camp out there, with sleeping bags on the floor."

Pete gave me his sad puppy-dog face. It was hard to be annoyed when he looked at me like that. Actually, from what I knew of his cousin Andy, the situation came as no surprise. Good guy. Bad luck. "And look where that act of kindness got him," I said, "not to mention where it got the deceased fencer or the folks here at New England Casualty and Indemnity. Tell me, how did this unfortunate fellow die? Smoke inhalation?" *Or would that make too much sense in this otherwise non-sensical scenario?*

"I'm afraid not, Ames. The guy was stabbed."

Triple damn! I stood and grabbed my coat and purse. "Let's go, Pete. I need to see this for myself. And check out the 'not extensive' damage before anybody around here gets wind of it. My job might hang in the balance."

I was probably exaggerating there, but you never know. A former co-worker came to mind. Her name was Judy Something-Or-Other. She had pulled all of her rather substantial weight to get Underwriting to accept a couple of questionable properties her family owned. Within a few months, each of them suffered a large loss. The next thing I knew, Judy was no longer employed at NEC&I. Maybe there was another reason for her departure, but the timing was suspicious.

Pete and I nearly collided with my assistant Peggy as she flew in the door of the outer office, her red hair windblown and even wilder than usual.

I said "Good morning, Peggy. Happy New Year. I've got to go."

She looked at her watch. "So soon? You'll miss the morning meeting. First meeting of the year. It might just be important, for a change."

I smiled at the thought. "Actually, I won't miss it at all."

"If you're not there, they'll probably talk about you. You know how these things go. Your old friend George will enjoy the chance to cast aspersions on your character." She hung her coat on a hook by the door and walked to her desk.

Aspersions be damned. I have work to do. "I hope they find something interesting, or at least entertaining, to say about me in my absence."

"What shall I tell them?"

"As little as possible. At least until I know more."

"About what?"

"There's been a fire. At Pete's cousin's place in Dorchester. I want to assess the damage. I'll call you when I have more news. In the meantime, mum's the word."

And I prayed whatever news I had wouldn't be too bad. This was not a good way to start the year.

CHAPTER 3

The legendary Boston traffic lived up to its reputation. Pete and I were at a standstill on Route 93 right before the entrance to the O'Neill tunnel. We'd been there for what seemed like ages. The perky fellow on the radio informed us there was an accident inside.

My usually laid-back and easy-going Pete wasn't taking the delay well at all. He banged his fist on the steering wheel and growled, "Dammit! I knew we should have taken Dorchester Avenue. Even with all those traffic lights, it would have been faster than this mess."

"I'm sure we'll be there shortly," I told him. "It looks like things are beginning to move up ahead."

"Sorry. I know I'm over-reacting. I'm just anxious to get there. Andy sounded bad on the phone, really beside himself. I'm worried about him."

Actually, I was glad for the delay. I needed the time to get my head on straight.

Pete turned to me. "What's up, Ames? You seem uneasy."

"I am."

"Because …?"

I paused for a moment, trying to put my feelings into words. "Because, in my long and occasionally illustrious career, I have investigated untold numbers of losses. But today is different. It's not just another fire or some storm damage. It's the scene of a death. I'm not sure how to handle that."

Pete gave me a sideways glance. "You've been to death scenes before and lived to tell the tale, haven't you?"

"Correct. And I've hated every one of them. But this time is different. The body is probably still there. And Andy's your cousin. The entire mess hits a lot closer to home. It's unsettling."

"Of course it is. You do know, though, that there's no way you'll get anywhere near the death scene until the body is removed and the entire area processed for evidence?"

"You're right. I do know that. I'll pull myself together for now, then perhaps fall apart whenever I finally gain access to the cellar where that poor fellow died."

It was time to change the subject. I needed to focus on something else. Anything else, actually. "I only met your cousin a few times. Tell me more about him. Are you two close?"

"He grew up next door to me in Newton. We were always best friends, despite the age difference. He's nearly ten years younger than me, not yet thirty. We became even closer after his father died. Andy was a quiet kid. Sensitive. Didn't have a lot of friends. I became somewhat of a surrogate father for Andy. Or at least an older brother. That's when I taught him to fence. I wanted to get him involved in something positive and fun."

"I'm guessing it worked."

"Sure did."

"If you two have been so close for so long, how come I didn't meet Andy until recently?"

"He spent the last few years on the West Coast. Only came home a few months ago. He had a girl out there, and a bad break-up. Whatever happened, he doesn't want to talk about it."

The traffic began to inch forward.

Pete advanced his car a few feet, then frowned. "Andy sunk everything he had into this rental property. I'd hate to see him lose it. In a way, I feel responsible for this disaster. I'm the one who encouraged him to become a landlord. He's always been handy. I felt it was a good career choice for him. And now this damn fire."

"That's what insurance is for, Pete. We'll take good care of him. I promise." I would make very sure that we did.

"Then there's the fellow who died. Andy's worried sick that somebody will find a way to blame him for it."

I didn't have an answer for that.

Twenty minutes later, we pulled up in front of the house at 12 Chadwick Street. The small residential neighborhood was total pandemonium, jam-packed with official vehicles – two police cars, a van labeled "Medical Examiner", another labeled "Crime Scene Investigations" and two fire trucks. Uniformed police, firefighters and a few men in suits crowded the sidewalk and front yard, both cordoned off with yellow police tape. Everybody was treading gingerly on the frozen ground. They walked in and out of the house through the space where the front door should have been and around the small front yard, all under the watchful eyes of some neighbors standing on their front porches in their slippers. Everybody was talking at once.

From the sidewalk, Andy's six-family wood-frame property looked relatively unscathed. It was a stereotypic Boston three-decker, painted brown with beige trim. Not an attractive house, but sturdy, solid. It had good bones. The area surrounding it was a sheet of ice. Apparently, the overnight temperature combined with water from the fire hoses had created a dangerously slippery situation.

"Why are the firefighters still here? Pete asked me. "Shouldn't the fire be out by now?"

"My guess is that they've been here all night," I told him. "Confirming that any hot spots are extinguished. With old wooden houses like this, you can't be too careful. Flames can spread from house to house really quickly."

We abandoned Pete's car on a side street and marched into the chaos. We spotted Pete's cousin Andy and joined him on the sidewalk across the street from his property. He looked cold and worried, and like he'd been up all night, which he probably had.

"Thanks for coming, guys." He gave Pete a brief man-hug, complete with the obligatory pats on the back. "This is all such a disaster. I don't know where to begin, or how. I'm worried sick about my tenants. I need to make sure they're all right, and someplace safe and warm."

"Have you been in touch with them?" Pete asked.

"I've been calling their cell phones since last night."

"And?" I questioned him.

"I located one of them. Ursula Fagan." Andy's voice quivered as he spoke. "She's at her daughter's home in Quincy. I've been trying to contact the other two, Ellen and Doug for hours. They're not answering their phones. I don't know what else to do, but it's important to find them. What if they have nowhere to go? I have to track them down in case they need help. They're my responsibility."

Andy's pain was palpable. I wasn't sure what I could do about it, but I'd think of something.

"My property's a mess," Andy continued. "I have no idea how bad the damage is. Could be a total loss for all I know. And that poor guy is dead. God, Pete, what am I going to do?" His eyes glistened with tears.

I answered for Pete. "You're going to take a deep breath and forge on. We'll deal with this together. One step at a time. Wait here with Pete and let me see what I can learn."

I switched my mind into insurance mode. Concentrating on the familiar and the mundane would help me hold it together. According to my job description, my primary interest in this loss was the fire damage. The deceased fencer could be an issue as well, though, and a very upsetting issue at that. We were also writing

11

liability coverage on the property. If the fellow's death could be blamed on Andy, he could be hit with a lawsuit which we'd need to defend and most likely pay. That was probably the worst case scenario.

I knew I couldn't enter the building to check out the damage today. Not with the multitude of officials bustling around doing their jobs. I was actually grateful for the delay. Still, I wanted to see what was happening and, with any luck, make a connection with the arson investigator or a police officer. It never hurt to have an in.

I approached a uniformed cop standing alone, taking in the scene and looking angry at the world. "Excuse me, please. Can you tell me who's in charge here? I'm going to need some information."

"I'm sorry, Ma'am," he snapped." You can't be here. This is an active crime scene."

"Actually, I need to be here." I handed him my business card. "My company insures this property. I have to assess the damage so we can begin working on the claim."

He looked doubtful.

I stared him down – one of my finer talents.

He acquiesced. "I guess that's all right, then. But make sure you don't get in anybody's way. And whatever you do, stay outside of the yellow tape."

"Do you know when the tape will come down?"

"When the crime scene techs are finished." He growled, then walked off to speak with somebody in a suit before I could ask him anything further.

I surveyed the scene and spotted a familiar face. An arson investigator I had worked with a few times in the past. Now if I could only remember his name. Something with a J. Jack? Jacob? Jared? Jimmy! That was it. Jimmy Landry. Tall, dark and handsome with curly hair and big brown eyes a girl could get lost in. Also a truly nice guy. A rare combination. He had wanted to date me a few years ago, but it was too soon after my fiancé Danny's death. I wasn't ready.

12

Then later, Pete came along, and the rest was history. I walked over and gave Jimmy my best smile. "Hello. Do you remember me?"

"Amy Lynch. Of course I remember you. I never forget a pretty face."

"Careful. That's my boyfriend over there." I pointed to Pete. Might as well let Jimmy know up front that I was unavailable.

"The one in the fancy suit?" Jimmy asked. "He looks like a lawyer on his way to court."

I smiled. "Good guess."

"Gotcha," Jimmy said. "So once again my timing is off. Who's that with him?"

"The owner of this property. He's Pete's cousin. His name is Andy Yesley."

"Poor guy looks like he's about to collapse. Or maybe cry. Something tells me you've got a personal interest here."

"Correct. But what can you do? It's also business. New England Casualty and Indemnity insures this property. I decided to handle this loss myself. My official concerns here are the cause of the fire and the extent of the damage, not to mention anything else I can learn about anything. What can you tell me?" *And let's not forget the body in the cellar.*

Jimmy closed his eyes for a moment, then said, "We haven't been able to do a thorough investigation yet. It's still too hot inside, but my guess is that it's not as bad as it could have been. Not as bad as it looks. The flames were confined to a portion of the cellar and the first floor apartment on the left. Good thing that apartment is unoccupied."

"Looks like we caught a break here," I said. *Hope sometimes does spring eternal.*

"That's for sure. Also, the firefighters got here quickly. That prevented the fire from growing out of control. Every minute counts in a fire, you know."

"That's for sure. If I remember correctly, fires double in size every sixty seconds."

"That's right," he said. Then he frowned. "Our biggest problem at this point is that the firefighters did their job well. They extinguished the fire in record time. And trampled all over the crime scene before they realized that's what it was.. Lord knows what evidence they may have corrupted."

"Does that mean the police won't be able to investigate?"

He shook his head. "No way. They'll do their usual thorough job and hope against hope that there is some viable evidence left."

"Were you able to get in at all?"

"Not yet. But the cops gave me a brief description of what they saw. The cellar has a packed-dirt floor and is apparently used only for storage, so there's no big problem there. And, as I said, only a portion of it was involved. The first floor apartment on the left has a lot of damage to the floor and walls. It's primarily smoke damage to the rest of the building. You know what that means. Everything's dirty. It doesn't smell good. Unpleasant, but not serious." He glanced up and down the street. "Actually, we got lucky. In an old neighborhood like this, with houses so close together, it's a wonder the whole street didn't go up in flames. Apparently the call came in before the fire got a chance to spread."

"Anything else I should know?" I asked.

"A couple of windows got blown out both in the cellar and on the first floor."

"From the fire?"

Jimmy shook his head. "More likely from the explosion."

I gasped. This was news. And not the good variety. "The what?"

He furrowed his brow. "Something in the cellar blew up. The woman next door said it sounded like fireworks. We're still trying to figure out what it was. The answer should lie somewhere down there. We'll find it."

My next question was: "Who called it in?"

"A neighbor." He pointed to a woman standing on the front porch of the three-family house next door.

I'd speak with her later. Maybe by then she'd be out of her robe and slippers.

"I know you're busy right now, Jimmy. Would it be all right if we spoke again later? Perhaps tomorrow? I think I'm going to have a lot of questions." *And with any luck, maybe he'd have learned something about the deceased fencer as well.* I wrote my cell phone number on the back of my business card and handed it to him.

"No problem, Amy. I'll give you a call tomorrow. By then we should have a better idea of what happened here."

I thanked Jimmy, then re-joined Pete and Andy shivering on the sidewalk. Standing together, they looked like Mutt and Jeff. Pete's six-foot two making Andy's five six or seven look even shorter. And Andy was as dark as Pete was fair. No one would ever guess they were related.

"Amy," Andy said, "thank you so much for being here for me. I don't know how to deal with any of this. First the fire. Then that poor fencer. I can't believe the guy is dead. This is awful. And, like I told you, two of my tenants are missing. I have to make sure they're all right." A tear ran down his cheek. He swiped at it with a trembling hand. "But I'll tell you one thing. I'm sure glad I bought that insurance when I did."

That made exactly one of us. As much as I wanted to help Andy, I was not looking forward to returning to my office and facing the fall-out from this debacle. There was no point in telling Andy that, though. He had enough to deal with at the moment.

Pete chimed in. "How about the three of us go someplace where we can talk? It doesn't look like we're going to learn much here at the moment. You looked wiped out, Andy. It'd be good for you to get out of the cold."

"Excellent idea," Andy said. "The Eire Pub is only a few blocks from here. We can get some lunch while we talk. And also warm up."

"Works for me," Pete said. "It's too cold to walk there, though. We can take my car. What about you, Ames? Are you in?"

"Absolutely."

CHAPTER 4

I loved the Eire Pub, a fixture in its Boston neighborhood for over 50 years. It has always been an interesting cross between a cozy local watering hole and a place for politicians – local and national – to gather and to be seen.

The sign outside proclaims the Eire as a Gentlemen's Prestige Bar. The interior screams old neighborhood pub, like one might find in Ireland. The bartenders dress in shirts and ties under their aprons, a nice little touch of class. Women have been welcome there for over thirty years now, though not because the establishment suddenly became enlightened. It was required by law. The pub also had to add a ladies' room. The menu is simple, good plain comfort food. It was the ideal place for the three of us to chat on this bleak January day.

Pete checked his wallet on the way in, then turned to me and Andy. "I hope one of you has some cash. No credit cards accepted here."

I looked in my own wallet. "Not to worry. I've got this covered."

We settled into a corner table. Pete and Andy ordered beers, though Andy looked like he could use something stronger. I stuck to hot tea. This was a working lunch. Besides, at the moment, I was chilled to the bone. Andy ordered a bacon cheeseburger with fries, also known as the cholesterol special. Pete and I both opted for turkey clubs, no fries. Might as well start the year out eating right.

Pulling out paper and pen, I turned to Andy. "OK. Start at the beginning. And please don't leave anything out."

The look on Andy's face suggested he wasn't sure where the beginning was. He chewed on his lower lip while he thought. "When I finally closed on the property last November, the weather wasn't right to begin a major rehab. And I wanted to come up with a little more money, to do the job properly. I had three vacant apartments. And my buddy Freddy – he's the fencing coach at McGill University – had a team of fencers coming down for the Hangover Open. They needed a place to stay, couldn't afford much. Most of the kids are on financial aid. It just made sense to let them camp out in my place."

"Tell me again what Freddy's last name is," I said, pulling out a notepad and pen.

"Dahlquist."

"How many fencers?"

"Eight. Two girls and six guys."

And one of them was now deceased. "How well did Freddy know these folks?" I asked.

"Well enough. He told me they were all good solid kids. Not to mention excellent competitive fencers, at least according to Freddy."

I made a few notes. "When did they arrive from Montréal?"

"Late in the afternoon on New Year's Eve. I met them at the house."

"How many keys did you give them?" I asked.

Andy avoided my eyes. "Actually none. The lock on the front door is busted. It happened the day before yesterday. I hadn't had a chance yet to get a locksmith over to look at it."

The look on Pete's face spoke volumes. "That could be a real problem. Anybody could have entered the building yesterday."

I bit my tongue as I considered this complication. "What happened after they arrived?"

"The team dropped off their stuff and headed to Linda Mae's for some dinner, then into town to celebrate First Night. I didn't see them again until yesterday morning, when they arrived at the fencing club."

"Were you at the tournament all day?"

"Of course. Wouldn't miss it for the world."

"What about Freddy and his team?" Pete wanted to know.

"That's hard to say," Andy replied. "I guess so, but there were over sixty fencers there. The Hangover Open always draws a good crowd. There aren't that many fencing events at this time of year. I know everybody fenced in the pools. That's the beginning of the tournament, Amy, when all fencers are divided into groups and each entrant fences each person in his group."

Pete broke in here. "You don't have to explain to Amy how a fencing tournament works. She's been a fan for years. Usually comes to my tournaments to cheer me on."

"That's good to know," Andy said. He turned to me. "After the pools, people were milling about all over, waiting for the results to be tabulated and the rankings posted. The weather was sunny. A lot of folks spent some time outside, despite the cold. Once the Direct Eliminations began, the crowd thinned out. As you probably know, a lot of fencers tend to leave a tourney once they've been eliminated."

"Are you really sure everybody on the team fenced in the pools?" I asked.

Andy responded. "Yup. I checked with Freddy."

Our sandwiches arrived. We were silent for a few minutes as the three of us dug into some tasty fare. Pete and I both helped ourselves to a few of Andy's fries.

When I came up for air, I asked Andy, "When did you learn of the fire?"

"Around the end of the Direct Eliminations. That must have been about 4:00 or 4:30. My cell phone rang. It was Helen Czwakiel from next door on Chadwick Street calling to let me know what was happening." A sheepish look crept across his face. "She also gave me the name of a local locksmith. I was planning to call him today. I guess there's no point now. The entire door needs to be replaced."

Pete gave him a funny look. "How did this woman get your cell number?"

"I gave it to her. The minute I met her, it was clear she was the quintessential nosy neighbor. It seemed like a good idea to have a contact 'on-site,' just in case something happened." He frowned. "But I never imagined anything would happen this soon. Or be this bad."

I asked him. "What did you do when you got her call?"

"I found Freddy and told him I had to leave, but that he and his team should stay at the fencing club until I had a better handle on what was happening. I figured nobody would be able to get back into the house any time soon."

"Did Freddy take a head count then?" I asked.

"He did. Everybody was there except Howie Zupkoff."

"Which means that must be Howie in the cellar?" I shuddered as I said this.

"Right. The name on his jacket confirmed it. And Freddy came by a while ago to make a positive ID for the police."

"What did the team do? Where did they spend the night?" Pete asked. I was glad he was with me. He was a good interrogator, didn't miss a trick. A lawyer through and through.

"At the Boston Fencing Club. They slept on the floor."

"I'm surprised the local members didn't take the team into their homes," I said.

"They offered," Andy replied. "The team didn't want to be split up. Apparently staying together helped them cope with Howie's death. Some of the local fencers supplied them with blankets or sleeping bags. Not too comfy, but at least it was warm. And the club has full washroom facilities, as well as a kitchenette. Definitely not all the comforts of home, but OK in a pinch."

"Why didn't they just camp out there in the first place?" I asked.

Pete responded to this. "It's technically against club policy. Otherwise, fencers from all over New England would be looking to stay there during tournaments. And that could cause a good deal of chaos."

I saw his point. It could also lead to a liability issue. "Where are Freddy's fencers now?"

"Still at the club," Andy said. "The police and fire officials want to speak with them as a group this evening. I'll be there as well. My plan is to bring pizzas so they can eat before the authorities arrive. Maybe that'll help distract them for a while. I was hoping you might join us, Pete. I could use the moral support."

"No problem," Pete said. "What time?"

"How about quarter to six? That'll give us time to eat before the police arrive at six-thirty. What about you, Amy? Will you join us?"

"Of course I'll come," I said. "Perhaps one of the kids saw or knows something that might explain why a member of their team ended up dead in Andy's cellar. In the meantime, let's talk about the building. And your tenants." I gathered my thoughts, then asked, "Six apartments, right?"

Andy. "That's right. Two on each floor."

"And three tenants at the moment?"

"Right."

"Who lives where?" I wasn't sure it mattered, but it was good to begin with all my ducks in a row.

"Ursula lives on the first floor right. Ursula Fagan. She's the one I was able to locate. At her daughter's in Quincy. She has been there off and on for a while now. Hasn't been well. I've actually only met her once. The first floor left apartment is vacant."

"That's a stroke of luck. From what I know so far, that's where the majority of the damage is. What about the second floor?"

"Both apartments are empty. That's where the fencing team camped out."

"So the other two tenants live on the third floor?"

"Ellen James on the left. Douglas Weiss on the right," Andy explained.

An odd look came over Andy's face. "You don't think either one of them is responsible for what happened?"

"I don't think anything at the moment," I told him. "These questions are just a formality. Besides, maybe I can help you track down the other two tenants."

"It'd be great if you did manage to find them." He made a sound somewhere between a sob and a sigh. "I feel so helpless. I can't just leave them out in the cold in January. And there's no telling when they'll be able to get back into the property." He let out a ragged breath. "I can't believe all this is happening. It's so awful."

"Hang in there, Andy," Pete told him. "You know Amy and I will both be there for you. We'll get through this together."

I remembered something I had heard earlier. "The arson investigator told me there was some kind of small explosion that may have contributed to the damage. Was there anything in the cellar which could have blown up?"

Andy shook his head. "Honestly, Amy, I just don't know. I barely paid any attention to the cellar. Too busy with the rest of the property, I guess. Sorry."

"And the prior owner didn't clean it out?" I asked.

"I thought he, or rather his estate, had." Andy's eyes teared up yet again. "I guess I should have checked. Now what should I be doing? There's so much to think about. And I've been so busy worrying about my tenants that I haven't even thought about the building. I don't know where to start."

"Leave that up to me," I told him. "Fire losses are common. We're good at handling them at NEC&I."

Andy looked doubtful. "Do you really think they'll give me enough money to make things right? After all, the building is old, and it wasn't in great shape to begin with."

"Do you remember that conversation we had when you bought the policy?" I reminded him. "About how you needed to buy enough coverage to rebuild from scratch in case of a major loss, not just enough to cover the current value of the house?"

That brought a small smile to his face. "Oh yeah. That's right. Does that mean I'll be all right as far as coverage goes?"

"I can't foresee any problems. We'll cover the cost to repair the building and also take care of the clean-up."

Andy's smile faded. "Geez, I hadn't even thought about clean-up."

"That's often the biggest issue after a fire. Smoke damage can be a bitch. And you'll need to get the front door and broken windows boarded up right away," I said. "Where is the second entrance to the building?"

"There's a rear door. Also a bulkhead in the back leading down into the cellar."

"Do they both lock?"

"The bulkhead is locked from the inside. The rear door is locked now as well."

"Do you have the key?" Pete asked.

Andy frowned. "I guess so. Someplace."

"Guessing isn't good enough," Pete continued. "You need to keep the place locked to keep out potential squatters. But other folks will need to get in, particularly the police. And while they won't let you actually enter the building until the crime scene is processed, they will have to let you work on the outside, taking measures to prevent further damage."

A visible bulb lit up on Andy's face. "How about I put a new lock on the back door? I can get it when I buy the plywood to board up the windows and the front door."

"Good idea," I said. "I'd like a key, if that's all right with you. And the police will need one as well."

"No problem," Andy replied. "I'll get on it this afternoon when I'm ordering a new front door and some windows."

"I can help you board things up," Pete said. "How about I check in with my office, change my clothes and meet you back on Chadwick Street in an hour or so?"

"Don't take this personally, Pal, but you've never been very handy. I'm not sure how much you can do to help."

"Not to worry. I'm actually pretty good with a hammer. You'll see."

"Then thanks. That'd be great." Andy relaxed visibly, then turned to me. "Is there anything else we need to talk about at the moment?"

"Not really," I told him. "I don't know what to think about the fatality. We'll have to wait and see how things play out with the police. I promise you I'll stay on top of it." *Whether I like it or not.*

Pete spoke up. "Perhaps we'll get some idea about that at the meeting this evening. And remember, you've got a competent attorney by your side if needed." He looked at his watch. "I'll drive you two back to Chadwick Street, then stop by my office."

I turned to Andy, "I walked to work this morning, then came here with Pete."

"So you'll be needing a ride to work in a while," he said.

"That's not necessary. I can take the T. Not my favorite mode of transportation, but it does the job. If you can drop me at the Red Line later, I'll be fine from there. But I want to revisit the fire scene first, even if I can't get into the building. Maybe there'll be some news."

I was eager to speak with Mrs. Czwakiel. Nosy neighbors are often a wonderful thing. And it'd be more pleasant speaking with her than facing the wrath of the Underwriting Department. I planned to delay that encounter for as long as possible.

CHAPTER 5

The chaos on Chadwick Street was still in full force. And the crowd of on-lookers had increased by at least half. People sure loved to gawk. A policeman called Andy over to speak with him, leaving me alone to see what I could learn. Two older women stood on the porch of the house next door observing the scene. One was stout and robust, with frizzy gray hair. She wore a plaid ankle-length coat and fuzzy pink slippers. The other woman was thin and frail, with a tight white bun. She was dressed in a black parka and boots. My guess was the woman in the slippers was Mrs. Czwakiel. I approached them and introduced myself.

"It's lovely to meet you," she said. "I'm Helen Czwakiel. And this is my good friend Beatrice Vaughn. She used to live next door."

"That's right," Beatrice said. "I moved a couple of months ago into Shady Oaks, that new assisted living complex around the corner. It's just a short walk from here and really quite nice. I would have preferred to stay here where I've always lived. I only moved there to keep my daughter happy. She worries about me."

That was probably more than I needed to know on the subject. Still, I smiled at her and feigned interest. It's always good to have a friend or two in the neighborhood.

"I'm hoping you ladies might have a few minutes to discuss the fire with me."

Beatrice looked at her watch. "I better be going. I really don't know anything. And my daughter is coming shortly to drive me to the eye doctor. She doesn't let me drive anymore. I take the bus from Shady Oaks when I need to shop. And I can walk here to visit with Helen. It all works out well enough."

Her words said one thing; the look on her face said another.

Mrs. Czwakiel smiled as her friend walked away. "All right, then, Bea. Be careful walking home. I'll call you in ten minutes to be sure you made it safely." She turned to me once Beatrice was out of earshot. "Her daughter is right to worry. Bea gets confused. She really shouldn't be out walking by herself." She looked next door. "What I don't understand is why the fire trucks and police are still here. Wouldn't you think the fire would be out by now?"

I repeated what I had told Pete earlier.

She looked doubtful, but didn't challenge my statement. "Andy is such a nice young man. Decent. Down to earth. And what a mess he's got on his hands. What can I do to help?"

That was my cue. "First, you could tell me everything you saw yesterday. Were you at home when the fire started?"

"I sure was. Like I already told the police, I had nowhere to go on New Year's Day. I stayed home and watched the parade on TV. Had just walked into the kitchen to make a cup of tea when all hell broke out next door."

"All hell?"

"You bet. The smoke detectors went off. One after another. They made quite a racket. Then there was a big bang from somewhere nearby. It sounded like somebody was setting off fireworks. I looked out the window and saw flames streaming out of the basement and first floor windows of number 12."

"Are you the one who called the fire department?"

"Sure am. Then I ran outside to make sure everybody got out of Andy's house real quick. The fire trucks arrived before I reached the front door. I couldn't believe how fast they were. Of course, the station is only a few streets away. And it was amazing how quickly they put the fire out. Unbelievable. At least I thought it was out."

"Did the tenants get out all right?" I hoped she'd know more about them than Andy did.

"Yes. I saw both Ellen and Doug dash out and head up the street somewhere. Ursula wasn't there. She's been staying with her daughter lately."

"Do you know where Ellen and Doug went?"

"Sorry, no. They just took off on foot in different directions. Neither of them owns a car."

I didn't know if that was good news or bad.

Mrs. Czwakiel gazed at the vehicles parked in front of the house then at the authorities coming around from the rear of the building. They were moving a gurney bearing what was obviously a body bag. "Wait a minute! If all the tenants got out safely, who do you suppose is in that body bag?"

That would be the late Howie Zupkoff. Unsure of what information the police were making public, I decided to keep that information to myself, at least for the moment.

A thought lit up on Mrs. Czwakiel's face. "I remember now. Andy had friends of his spending a few days here. Some sort of team here for a tournament."

"A team of fencers."

"Right. Fencers. I met a few of them when they arrived yesterday. They brought swords with them. Seemed like nice young folks. Oh dear! Do you suppose it's one of them they're bringing out?"

"I really couldn't say."

She seemed to accept that answer, so I didn't have to lie.

We both fell silent as we observed the somber scene. Moving the gurney through the icy yard proved to be a tricky process – and slow. Then all pandemonium ceased for a moment as they loaded the body into the medical examiner's van. Several onlookers bowed their heads when the gurney passed them.

Mrs. Czwakiel made the sign of the cross. "Such a shame."

I couldn't disagree. "What can you tell me about the tenants?" Based on what Andy said, odds were she'd know something useful.

She wrinkled her brow. "Well, Ursula is a nice lady. She has lived there for years, almost as long as I've been here. She had to retire a few years ago and go on disability. Poor thing was beginning to have trouble getting around. MS. Had to move from her second floor apartment down to the first floor. She has been in and out of the hospital lately. Also spent some time in rehab. Like I said, she's at her daughter's right now. My guess is she'll stay there."

That agreed with what Andy had said.

"Do you know her daughter's name?"

"I should. I used to. Can't think of it at the moment, though. Sorry." She closed her eyes for a second. "Then there's this girl in her twenties. Her name is Ellen. Ellen James, I believe. I'm not so fond of her. She has no use for an old lady like me. Doesn't even have the common decency to say hello. She usually looks in the other direction if I pass her on the street. Not only that, but the girl comes and goes at all hours of the day and night. She certainly doesn't seem to work regular hours. If she works at all, which I doubt. And she has tattoos all up and down her arms. Can you believe that? Not only that, but she's got this boyfriend. The boy gives me the creeps. He hangs around there a lot. Sure looks to me like the two of them are up to no good."

"Do you know his name?"

She shook her head. "Sorry. I wish I did."

"What about the third tenant?" I checked my notes. "Douglas Weiss. Do you know him?"

"Not very well. He moved in about three months ago. Just before Andy bought the place. Doug looks to be in his forties. He seems like a decent sort. Always says hello. Very polite. He comes and goes on a regular schedule. That probably means he has a steady job. Doing what, I don't know. He's not much on conversation."

I gave Mrs. Czwakiel my card, writing my cell number on the back. "If you think of anything else, or see something suspicious, can you please let me know?"

She took the card in her hand, extended her arm and squinted. "You've got it. I'm happy to help in any way I can."

"You already have." And I hoped she'd be the gift who keeps on giving – if she could manage to read my card.

As I started to walk away, she called me back. "Wait a second. There he is. Douglas Weiss. Over there in the green pea coat." She pointed to a fellow standing on the sidewalk looking scruffy and sad. He was on the short side, with longish brown hair under a faded Red Sox cap, a full beard and sunglasses.

I walked over and introduced myself.

"Pleased to meet you," he said. "Do you have any idea how bad the damage is here? The cops and the firefighters won't tell me anything."

I shook my head. "Sorry. It's too early to know for sure."

"I'm really anxious to get back in. I've got nowhere else to go. I stayed last night at the motel on Gallivan Boulevard, but I can't afford that for long. And I can't move someplace else either. Most landlords around here want a security deposit and first and last months' rent. I don't have that kind of money." He gave me an embarrassed smile.

"Let me see what I can do," I told him. "I have an in with your landlord." I gave him my card and took his cell number.

I watched Weiss as he walked off in the direction of Gallivan Boulevard. Mrs. Czwakiel was right. He seemed like a nice guy who was down on his luck. His shoes needed heels and his pants were shiny. Sometimes appearances can be deceiving, though. You just never know.

The firemen and the forensic team were still busy at work. I spotted Jimmy Landry, the arson investigator, coming toward me.

"Any news?" I asked him.

"One thing that may interest you. The cause of the small explosion. I probably shouldn't be telling you this until we know more. Right now I'm not even sure how it fits in."

That sounded ominous. "What was it?"

"Ammunition."

"As in bullets?"

"Right. Big ones. Bigger than the bullets that the cops use. They were impressed. The stuff was just beginning to blow when the firefighters found it. If the entire box had been set off, it could have caused one hell of an explosion."

Oh my. That was a major complication. Definitely not good news.

"So the fire caused the bullets to ignite, not the other way around, right?" I asked.

"Correct. And I'm actually shocked that it happened at all. It takes a pretty hot fire to set ammo off. I'm wondering if perhaps some of the bullets had degraded somehow and spilled their guts onto the ground. I'll need to check that out."

"And keep me posted?" I reminded him.

"Sure thing." He flashed me a killer smile. If not for Pete, I could develop a serious fondness for this guy. But not now. I was not going there.

Andy returned from conferring with the authorities and drove me to the T station. Along the way, I questioned him about the ammunition in the cellar.

"Holy crap!" he responded. "This is awful. What the hell were bullets doing down there? Isn't it against the law to keep ammunition around like that? What if the police think it was mine? Which it isn't. I don't have a firearms license. I could be in big trouble."

I had no good response for him.

Andy dropped me at the Ashmont Station. The Boston MBTA, or the T as we call it, was the country's first subway system. And at least some of the original tunnels under Boston Common were still in use. I didn't know if that made me feel proud of our fair city or slightly uneasy.

CHAPTER 6

I was uneasy enough as it was, wondering about the greeting I might get back at the office. The last thing I needed right now was a conversation with George. Hoping to delay my return as long as possible, I popped into my apartment, which was only a few blocks from the office, to take my dog Sam for a walk. I rationalized that he needed the fresh air and exercise. With the cold weather we'd been having lately, we'd been taking short walks. He deserved better. The walk would give me time to organize my thoughts about how to downplay the fire damage to the powers that be at work. It'd be hard to downplay the deceased fencer.

Sam's entire body wagged when I opened the door. I was pretty sure he could tell time and knew that I wasn't really supposed to be home so early in the afternoon. He ran to his leash and gave me his best doggie grin.

"Come on, Buddy. Let's go."

We walked to the park near the Courthouse. I filled Sam in on the events of the day. He was a wonderful listener. As we stood waiting for a few cars to pass so we could cross First Street, Sam strained at his leash to inspect something on the sidewalk. The next thing I knew, he was scarfing down whatever treat he had found. It was a bad habit of his I was struggling to break. Obviously with little success.

"Sam! Don't you dare eat that. You don't know where it's been."

I was too late. He was licking his lips, as well as the wrapper of a high-end chocolate bar. And he was smiling, oblivious to the dreadful things that chocolate does to dogs. I grabbed my cell and called the vet.

"Amy! It's great to hear from you. It's been far too long. How are you doing?"

"I'm fine, Henry, but I'm sorry to say this is not a social call." I gave him the details of Sam's misadventure.

"Bring him in right away," Henry said. "And plan for him to spend the night with us. Ingesting chocolate can be fatal to dogs. We'll need to pump his stomach then monitor him for at least twelve hours."

Fatal! Please, no! Not my Sam. "We'll be there right away."

"And don't worry, Amy. We'll take good care of him. Sam will be just fine."

I prayed that Henry was right, as I hurried home and got Sam into my Mustang. "Not to worry, Buddy," I told him. "Doc Henry says you're going to be all right." I scratched behind his ears as I headed off, frantic to get Sam help as quickly as possible.

I needed to calm down and think clearly. I knew that Henry would take good care of Sam, but I sill couldn't help worrying. I did what I could to keep my mind busy and free of worry. I called Peggy.

I knew I shouldn't dial while driving, but the traffic was slow enough that it wasn't much of an issue. Besides, I put the phone on speaker and stood it in the cup holder.

"Well it's about time! I've been worried sick. Where are you, Amy? Is everything all right? How bad was the fire?"

"I'll tell you about that later. Something else has come up. I'm with Sam. He ate a chocolate bar he found on the sidewalk and is about to become seriously ill. We're on our way to the vet now." It pained me to say that out loud.

"Oh, no. That's terrible. Please tell me he's going to be OK."

All I could say was, "I hope so."

"I'm guessing this means you'll be really late getting to the office, right? Don't worry. I'll hang around until you get here."

"Afraid not, Peg. Sorry."

"And that's because ...?"

"Because I'm in Cambridge and the vet is in Dorchester. It'll take me the best part of half an hour to get there with the traffic this time of day. Not to mention the drive back to Cambridge right when the afternoon rush is at its worst." *Also not to mention that I wanted to avoid announcing the fire loss to my co-workers until I had a better idea of the situation. That would be sometime tomorrow.*

"Dorchester is rather inconvenient for you, isn't it? Why in the world do you use a vet so far from where you live?"

Good question, but an easy one to answer. "He's an old friend, a friend of Danny's actually. The vet had already checked Sam out when Danny gave him to me." Sam had been a Christmas gift from my late fiancé Danny. The last gift he gave me before he died. I didn't have the heart to change vets. It was one of my few remaining connections to Danny. As much as I cared for Pete, I wasn't ready to let Danny go completely. Not just yet. Maybe never.

Stroking Sam's head as I drove, I asked Peggy, "How did the meeting go?"

"You mean are you in major hot water?"

"Exactly."

Peggy seldom minced words with me, though she always had my back.

"Not to worry," she said. "Not yet. I didn't mention the fire to them, if that's what you're asking. What they don't know can't hurt you. I thought it would be wise to wait and see how bad the damage was before throwing you under the Underwriting bus."

I breathed a little easier. "Thank you for that. You've earned your pay for the week and then some. What did you tell them to explain my absence?"

"That you had an emergency and you'd probably be in later. I did my best to make it seem like it was none of their business."

"Which it isn't. How did they react to that?"

"George tried to make a big deal out of it, but nobody paid much attention to him."

"Nobody ever does."

Peggy laughed. The girl was a gift from Heaven, always ready to cover my ass when I couldn't do so myself. I didn't know what I'd do without her. "Tell me what was discussed at the meeting. Was there anything worth noting?"

"Not really. Just the usual pep talk about 'Let's make this the best year ever at good old New England Casualty and Indemnity,' followed by a litany of statistics meaningful only to an actuary."

"Sounds like I dodged a bullet."

"Yeah. A really big one."

Like the bullets in Andy's cellar? "I will be in later," I told her. "But it's going to be later in the week, as in tomorrow. Sam needs to spend the night in the hospital. I will pick him up as soon as the vet opens in the morning, bring him home and then get to the office as soon as I can."

"Can I do anything for you in the meantime?"

"That is the other reason for my call. As much as I hate to do it, we do need to get this claim up and rolling. Andy needs the money as quickly as possible."

"Not that I'm not delighted to help you, but you do know you can do that from home."

Peggy was constantly appalled by my lack of interest in the latest technology. Not to mention my extreme paucity of skills.

"I could if I had my laptop with me." I told her. "When I left the office this morning, I never even thought about bringing it with me. Of course, I assumed I'd be back in before the end of the day."

"Understood. Tell me what you've got."

I gave her the bare bones information, which truly was all that I had. "No hard news yet on the cause of the fire or the cause of death. Hopefully I'll know more tomorrow." No point in mentioning the exploding ammunition until I had a few more facts.

"Sounds good. I'll get this set up right away."

"There is one more thing." I drove with one hand and fished through my purse for my notes with the other.

"Which is?"

I gave her the names of Andy's three tenants. "Can you run these folks through every database available? I need to know everything you can learn about them. Just in case one of them had a reason to start the fire."

"Or kill that poor fencer."

I groaned. "Thanks for reminding me. Anyway, get Tiffany to work on this with you. It'll be good experience for her."

"Got it," she said. "Let's hope we find something interesting." Peggy was nothing if not inventive, one of the many reasons I relied on her so much. If there was dirt to be found on any of the tenants, she would surely find it.

I disconnected the call and scratched Sam's head. Poor guy had no clue how unpleasant his next several hours would be.

I hit the gas pedal hard and maneuvered my way through the traffic. I needed to get Sam settled at the vet, then return home to change for the meeting with the police at the fencing club. With any luck, somebody there, police or fencers, might shed some light on how Howie Zupkoff's body ended up in Andy's cellar.

CHAPTER 7

P ete picked me up at 5:30 and we drove to the Boston Fencing Club. The club had recently relocated to the old Boston Globe building on Morrissey Boulevard in Dorchester. It was one of the few places in Greater Boston that had decent parking. Always a plus.

Andy pulled into the parking lot right after us. "Hey, Pete. Can you give me a hand with the pizzas?"

Pete dashed over to help him unload the pizza boxes from the van.

I carried the soft drinks and cookies.

Coach Freddy met us at the door. He was tall and thin, with curly blond hair and a worried look on his face. Andy handled the introductions.

"Thanks for coming, folks," Freddy said. "This is going to be tough on the kids. Being interviewed by the police is scary. Particularly on top of everything else that has happened. I'll take all the help I can get."

"How are the kids doing?" I asked.

Freddy frowned. "About what you'd expect. They're just kids, all of them under twenty. They're in shock. For most of them, this is their first experience with death. The reality of it hasn't sunk in yet.

Or the finality." He stifled a sob. "I'm doing my best to be strong for them, but inside I'm falling apart."

Andy squeezed Freddy's arm. "Hang in there, man. We're here for you."

We followed Freddy into the club. He clapped his hands to get the team's attention. "Listen up, guys. Pizza is here, compliments of my friend Andy, his cousin Pete and Pete's friend Amy."

The kids murmured their thanks.

"We're sorry about your teammate," I said. "This must be terribly hard for all of you. We're here to help in any way we can."

Pete added, "We can only imagine what you're going through. Please, whatever you need, don't be afraid to ask."

Freddy turned to us. "This is my team. He waved an arm toward the group of fencers, four guys and two girls, He pointed to each fencer as he spoke. "This is Michelle, Gina, Richie, Eric, TJ, Wyatt…" He stopped dead and stared.

"What's wrong?" Pete asked.

A visibly-shaken Freddy replied "Somebody's missing. There should be seven of them." He wrinkled his brow and stared at his team. "It's Bob. He isn't here. Where the heck could he be?"

Everybody gasped and looked around.

"Maybe he just went to the bathroom or something," a red-headed fellow suggested.

The guy next to him shook his head. "Nope. I just left there. Didn't see him."

"When was the last time any of you saw him?" Freddy asked.

A petite blonde girl spoke up. "He was here at lunchtime. I'm sure of that because he spilled his Gatorade all over me. Such a clumsy jerk."

A mousey girl with thick glasses gave her a dirty look.

The blonde continued. "I had to change my shirt. And the only thing I had to change into was my fencing jacket because all of our stuff is back at the house."

"Hasn't anybody seen Bob since lunch?" Freddy asked.

All six fencers shook their heads.

Freddy turned to us. "Oh my God. This is awful. It can't be true. It just can't be. I'm responsible for these kids. We've got to find him. What am I going to do?"

Pete spoke up. "You're going to pull yourself together and try to stay calm. The police will be here soon. They'll help."

Freddy nodded, but if his shaking hands were any indication, he was far from calm.

"And in the meantime," I added, "you folks all need to eat something. I'm sure you don't feel much like it, but you still need to keep up your strength."

A couple of fencers made their way to the table where the pizzas were set up.

I whispered to Pete and Andy, "Time for us to mingle. I'll chat with the girls. You guys take the boys. Let's try to draw them out. Talking helps. And one of them might know something helpful."

The two girls weren't heading to the pizza table. I walked over to them. "You ladies really should try to eat something."

The mousey-looking girl shook her head. "I can't. I don't know how anybody could eat at a time like this."

I knew what she meant. "I'm sure this is difficult for you folks. I'm so sorry for everything you're going through. First one of your teammates is dead and now another one is missing. Not to mention the fire at the house and having to camp out here. There's nothing good about any of it. And sometimes it's hard to be strong."

The little blonde girl burst into tears. "Sorry," she said. "I can't help it."

I patted her hand. "It's OK. Crying helps. You need to let it out somehow."

She stared at the floor "I know, I know. But you don't understand."

"Understand what? Am I missing something?"

She sniffled. "The worst thing of all."

"And what's that? It's all right to tell me, you know. I'm here to help."

Her teammate spoke up. "The reason we feel so bad is because nobody really liked Howie. He was odd. We weren't very nice to him. And now he's dead."

The blonde girl lowered her eyes. "And it's too late to change things. We should have been nicer. We could have been. And now we can't."

"And Bob is gone too. Disappeared. This is all so awful."

"I know it is," I told them. "But please eat something. Before the police get here."

They frowned, but did as I suggested.

I wandered over to where Pete and Andy were sitting with the boys. "Hi, guys," I said. "I'm very sorry about your troubles, losing your teammate, then being stuck here at the fencing club. What have you been doing to pass the time?"

A tall blond fellow spoke up. "Coach Freddy has been keeping us plenty busy. Putting us through our paces. Sparring. Working out. It helps."

"That's good to hear," I said. "And Freddy's right. Being busy does help. So does talking."

Nobody responded to that.

I watched in mild amazement as the male contingent of the team consumed most of the pizzas, eight of them, in record time. Apparently fencing was good for working up an appetite, at least where the guys were concerned. I took one of the two remaining slices and watched the fencers. They seemed like good kids. I wondered if any of them had opened up to Andy and Pete.

CHAPTER 8

The police arrived as we were disposing of the dinner trash. An official-looking gray-haired man in an ill-fitting blue suit, two police officers and a uniformed firefighter. My friend Jimmy, the arson investigator, was absent. Maybe he was busy elsewhere. Maybe he had nothing of interest to discuss. Yet.

Freddy made the introductions, indicating that Pete was Andy's lawyer. The detective eyed me curiously. "From the insurance company, huh? So what brings you here tonight? We're looking into the fatality, you know, not the fire."

"They may well be related," I said. "I like to leave no stone unturned." And that was all he needed to know.

The detective shrugged. "Whatever you say. Just don't get in our way."

"Good evening, everybody," the man in the suit addressed the group. "I'm Detective Frank Donnelly. This is Officer Flaherty, Officer Mankin and Fire Chief Molloy." Donnelly shifted from one foot to the other. "We want to thank you folks for meeting with us at a time like this. I know how difficult it must be for you. I'll do my best to make this as painless as possible. Please accept my condolences on the tragic death of your teammate."

The fencers stared at him in silence.

Freddy spoke up. "And now we've got another team member missing."

The detective's eyes grew wide. "What's that? Good grief. Exactly what is going on around here?"

Freddy frowned. "I wish I knew. All I can tell you is that Bob has turned up missing. Nobody remembers seeing him since lunch time. I don't know what to do."

Donnelly began making notes. "Let's take this one step at a time. What's this guy Bob's last name?"

"Poirier" Freddy told him. "Robert Poirier."

"What can anybody tell me about him?" Donnelly asked.

The six fencers all stared straight ahead in silence.

"Come on, folks. Somebody has to know something," Donnelly prodded.

The mousey girl with glasses raised her hand. "I have something to tell you. I don't know if it'll help or not. Yesterday, when I got eliminated, I went outside for some fresh air. There were a lot of people out there. Including Howie and Bob."

Officer Flaherty interrupted, "Meaning the recently deceased Mr. Zupkoff and the currently missing Mr. Poirier?"

"Right. They were having some kind of argument. I couldn't hear what they were saying, but they both sure sounded angry. Then Howie stormed off in a huff."

"What did Poirier do next?"

She shrugged. "I don't know. I went back inside."

"And nobody has seen him since lunch today?" Officer Flaherty asked.

"Actually I did," the mousey girl admitted. "I saw him leaving the building an hour or so ago. I ran after him and called his name. I guess he didn't hear me, because he kept on walking."

Detective Donnelly frowned at her. "Why didn't you tell somebody right away?"

I wondered the same thing.

The girl cringed. "Because I didn't want to get Bobby in trouble. Coach Freddy told us not to leave."

"Which direction did he take?"

She pointed out the window to the South East Expressway.

Detective Donnelly turned his head to Officer Mankin, who headed toward the door. "Gotcha," Mankin said. "I'll get right on it."

The detective watched him go, then said. "Let's move on from Mr. Poirier for the moment. Until we see what Officer Mankin is able to learn. In the meantime, what can any of you tell me about the late Mr. Zupkoff? What was he like? How well did you know him? Was he popular? Friendly? A good fencer?"

His questions were met with silence. He glared at them. "There's got to be something you can tell me about the guy."

Coach Freddy intervened. "Come on, folks, tell the police what you were saying to me earlier. It's important."

"And the sooner you do, the sooner I can get out of your hair," Donnelly added.

That remark did the trick. Amid a flurry of moans and groans, all six team members replied at once.

"Nobody really knew Howie all that well. He was new to the team."

"And not very out-going. Kept to himself most of the time."

"Not a team player."

"Gave the impression he thought he was better than the rest of us."

"Well, he was a better fencer."

Pete spoke up here. "Is that right, Freddy?"

"He was a very strong fencer, perhaps even gifted. We were lucky to have him on the team." Freddy looked around the room. Nobody contested his statement.

"And yet he was eliminated early in the tournament on Sunday," one of the fencers said. "What was up with that?"

42

Interesting question. And nobody seemed to have an answer.

Donnelly scribbled notes furiously. "Anything else?"

"I hate to speak ill of the dead, but Howie was kind of creepy," the mousy girl said. "Always poking around where he had no business being. He liked to sneak up behind people and scare them. Weird things like that. Last night I saw him skulking around the house where we're staying. Coming out of one of the first floor apartments and heading toward the cellar stairs. He was carrying his weapon. Weird."

Donnelly's head shot up from his notebook. "Hold it right there. What's this about a weapon? Are you telling me this guy was armed?"

Coach Freddy responded, "She means his fencing weapon. It was an épée. They have a rounded tip. Definitely non-lethal."

Donnelly made some notes. "Do all fencers use épées?"

"No," Freddy told him. "Some use foils and sabers."

"What's the difference?" Donnelly asked.

"They're used differently. Each weapon comes with its own set of rules of engagement. Épée is the most commonly used. Épée competition is the purest form of fencing," Freddy said. "It has fewer complications, fewer rules. First one to draw blood wins."

Donnelly frowned. "Please tell me you don't mean that literally."

"Of course not," the coach replied.

The detective looked bemused, but didn't follow up on this information. Instead, he turned back to the mousy girl and asked, "When you saw Mr. Zupkoff last night heading toward the cellar, did you question him about what he was doing?"

She stared past Donnelly. "I did. He mumbled something about looking for a washing machine. Like he wanted to do his laundry or something. How weird is that? And why would he need his épée to do laundry?"

Donnelly shook his head. "I guess we'll never know."

"He was acting weird at the tournament yesterday morning too," the girl continued. "I mean, even weirder than usual. I actually wondered if he might be high on something."

Donnelly pursed his lips and made some more notes. "Let's talk about the tournament yesterday. My first question is why do you call it the Hangover Open?"

Pete chuckled. "Two reasons. It always takes place on New Year's Day and the trophy has a dog on it, about 10 inches tall, wearing a plaid bathrobe and holding an ice bag to its head."

Donnelly gave Pete a curious look, then asked the group. "What time did you folks arrive at the tournament?"

"Early," Freddy told him. "Just after 8:00. Staying so close to the club, it was a quick and easy ride."

"How did you get here?"

"We took both our SUVs," Freddy said. "Fencing equipment takes up a lot of room."

Donnelly made a note. "Who rode with Mr. Zupkoff?"

Five hands went up.

"Did he say or do anything out of the ordinary?"

The tall blonde fellow replied to this. "Not really. He was just really quiet. Off somewhere in his own strange little world."

"What time did the tournament begin?" Donnelly asked

"Just after 9:00," Freddy replied. "The pools lasted a little less than two hours."

"Pools?" Donnelly asked.

Andy explained, "That's the opening round. There were sixty-four fencers registered. They were divided into ten pools, six or seven fencers to a pool. Each of them fenced with everybody else in his or her pool."

Donnelly took copious notes. "Then what?"

"Then the tournament officials took about half an hour to tabulate the results of the pools and post the rankings" Freddy told him. "That was unusual. Normally this takes about ten minutes, but they had a problem with the laptop not booting up and they had to do it manually."

"What did the fencers do while this was happening?"

"Mostly milled around, hung out with their teammates. Sparred a little. Had something to eat. I think I saw one fellow napping," Freddy said.

Officer Flaherty spoke up. "Did anybody leave the building during this time?"

Freddy didn't even need to think about that. "Yeah. A lot of fencers went out for some fresh air. The day had warmed up a little by then. Besides, it smelled like a locker room in here."

"Any of you folks go out?" Flaherty asked the team.

The pretty blonde girl spoke up. "I did."

"Did you see anything unusual out there?"

"Nope. Sorry."

I wondered why she'd bothered to speak up at all.

Donnelly consulted his note. "Once the rankings were posted, what happened next?"

"The DEs," Freddy replied.

"DEs?"

"Right," Freddy said. "Direct Eliminations. In this round, individual matches are assigned according to rankings, the higher ranked fencers paired against those with lower results. Whoever loses this match is eliminated from the competition. Hence the name."

The cops gave him a bemused look.

"It works something like the March Madness basketball tournament," Pete explained. "Of the original sixty-four fencers, thirty-two were eliminated in the first DE round. Then sixteen in the next round, then eight, and so on."

"Gotcha," Donnelly said.

"These fencers who are eliminated, what do they do?" Donnelly asked.

"It depends," Freddy told him. "Some leave, usually with discouraged looks on their faces. Others hang around to watch the final matches, root for their teammates."

"Getting back to Mr. Zupkoff, somebody said he was eliminated early?" Donnelly asked.

Freddy responded, "Right. In the first DE round, as a matter of fact. That was not at all like him. He usually fares much better. Apparently poor Howie was having a bad day."

And it only got worse from there. Poor guy indeed.

"Did he hang around to watch the finals?"

The six fencers and Freddy looked at each other. Nobody seemed to recall seeing him after his losing match.

"Is it possible he left?" Donnelly asked.

"Could be," the red-headed fencer spoke up. "He was coming down with a cold. Said he wasn't feeling very well. And he kept talking about his laundry. I mean, really, the guy was obsessed with his dirty socks."

I had a question. "Any thoughts on how Howie ended up back on Chadwick Street?"

"He could've walked there," Freddy said. "It's only a few blocks from here."

I thought about this. "Would he have known the way?"

"Actually he could have," the blonde girl said. "He told me he grew up around here. Somewhere in South Boston."

Detective Donnelly stood quietly. The look on his face suggested serious thinking. Finally, he announced, "OK, folks, here's what we're going to do. Officer Flaherty here is going to pass out paper and pens. I need each of you to write down exactly what you just told me. And anything else you can think of. Don't leave anything out. And make it legible, please. Then sign your statement. I'll check them over before I leave tonight to see if I'll have any additional questions for you."

Flaherty reached into a box he had with him and began to pass out the supplies.

While the kids were writing their statements, Pete questioned the Fire Chief and Detective Donnelly. "Do you have any idea what started the fire?"

"Nothing definitive yet." Molloy responded.

Maybe that explained why my friend Jimmy the arson investigator wasn't here.

"What about the cause of death?" Pete continued. He was beginning to sound like he was conducting a cross-examination.

"Nothing definitive," Donnelly said.

Pete rolled his eyes in my direction.

I pretended not to notice.

When the statements were completed and handed in, the little blonde girl said, "I hate to sound self-centered here, but we really do need to know what to expect. Do you have any idea when we'll be able to get back into the house? All our stuff is there."

Officer Flaherty said, "As soon as we're done processing the crime scene and the building has been certified safe. Unless we run into any complications, you can probably retrieve your belongings in a day or two. We'll keep you posted."

That announcement brought on a loud collective groan. I felt sorry for the kids. Not a good way to end their winter break. I decided not to mention that when they did get their belongings back, everything would reek of smoke. No sense overburdening them yet.

A slightly overweight fellow spoke up, "You know, we do need to get home soon. Classes will be starting up again. And exams are coming."

Somebody added, "That's for sure. I'm practically flunking out as it is."

That provided a small break in the tension.

"We're doing the best we can," Detective Donnelly told them. "We know it's a tragedy for you all, and an inconvenience, but there's a lot going on here, and we need to be thorough. Now let me take a look at your statements."

CHAPTER 9

Back in the car, Pete said to me, "Well, that was interesting. So let's review things. What did we learn here?"

I provided a short list off the top of my head. "Howie Zupkoff was a good fencer but, for some reason, his game was off yesterday. He was also a misfit. Nobody liked him. Nobody knows why he left the tournament, or exactly when. Also, he was behaving oddly."

I came up for air while Pete digested this information, then added, "And that girl with the glasses probably has a crush on Robert Poirier."

"What makes you say that?"

"The dirty look she gave the blonde girl who called him a clumsy jerk. And at first she didn't tell anybody Poirier had left because she didn't want to get him in trouble."

Pete seemed to accept my reasoning.

"What else? Oh, yes. Zupkoff and Poirier had a disagreement. Zupkoff left angry, probably walked back to Chadwick Street. Apparently, he knew the way."

"Why did he go into the cellar?" Pete asked. "Do you really think he wanted to do some laundry? Why did he bring his épée with him? And how did he end up dead?"

48

"Also how did the fire start?" I added. "My investigation hinges on that."

"We have a chicken and egg scenario here," Pete said. "Was Howie killed, then the fire started to cover that up ...?"

I finished the thought for him, "Or did Howie start the fire and somebody kill him for it? And if so, who might that somebody be?" I didn't know which had come first, but I was convinced the two events were connected.

"What did you think of that fire chief?" Pete asked. "I'm not sure why the man was there. He hardly said a word."

"Maybe his assignment was to observe the fencers, trying to spot anybody with a guilty look on his face."

Pete turned toward me, eyes wide. "Amy Lynch, in all the time I've known you, I never knew you had such a suspicious mind."

"In my job that's an asset. And don't you ever forget it." I winked to let him believe I might be kidding. "Eyes back on the road, Buddy. By the way, how did you and Andy do boarding up the broken door and windows?"

"It's all buttoned up tight now. Front door and blown-out windows all secured. The rear door is all set as well. I have a key for you. Andy has one for the police. And despite what Andy said about my carpentry skills, I was a big help."

We finished the trip to my apartment in companionable silence.

Pete groaned as he pulled up in front of my building. "This has been a hell of a way to start the year. Please tell me it can only get better from here."

I took his gloveless hand in mine. "You look frazzled, Pete, like you could use a little R & R. There happens to be a lovely bottle of Korbel chilling in my fridge. Any interest in sharing it with me? To wash down all that pizza?"

He gave me his best phony leer. "Might that invitation also include some fooling around?"

"It might." I fluttered my eyelashes at him.

"Let's go."

The first thing that hit me as I entered my third-floor apartment was that my pal Sam wasn't there to greet me. Poor little guy. I'd miss him tonight. I knew Henry would take good care of Sam, but that didn't stop me from worrying. I was glad Pete was there with me. I didn't feel like being alone.

I listened to my voicemail messages while Pete wrestled with the champagne cork. My parents checked in from their journey south. They were spending the night outside of Philadelphia. Everything was going fine. They'd be at my sister's in Baltimore tomorrow and would spend the night there. I hoped that next year they'd ship the car down to Florida and take a plane. I worried about them doing a multi-day road trip at their age.

There was a message from Peggy, asking me to call her at home no matter what time it was. I followed her instructions and prepared myself for what could only be bad news.

"What's happening, Peggy?" *And please break it to me gently.*

"I wanted to give you a heads-up before you get to the office tomorrow. George is on the warpath. Big time. Or maybe in his glory. Could be either, or perhaps both. He went berserk when he learned about the fire, in that oh-so-very smug way of his."

I was well acquainted with George's smugness. It was one of his least pleasant attributes. One among many. "Bad news certainly travels fast at New England Casualty and Indemnity."

"That's for sure," Peggy said. "Seeing you in potential trouble seemed to make George's day. What did you ever do to the man to make him dislike you so much?"

"I did my job," I told her, "and sometimes part of his as well. How did he find out about the fire?"

"It was sort of my fault, I guess. Or maybe just a fluke. A really unfortunate fluke. And I'm sorry. I couldn't stop him. The man came strutting into my office looking for you when I was setting the claim up in the system. He actually stood behind me and read my computer screen. He didn't even try to look casual about it. Then he gave me that evil smirk of his and said, 'Heads are gonna roll when the folks in Underwriting hear about this. I warned them it was a bad idea. They knew they shouldn't take on that property, but they did it anyway, as a favor to the illustrious Ms. Lynch. Looks like it's turning out to be a very expensive favor.' Then he strolled off into the proverbial sunset."

"He does realize that I'm his boss, not the other way around, right?"

Peggy laughed. "Some days it's hard to tell. Anyway, that's the scoop from NEC&I. I thought you should know before you get here in the morning. I wish you luck with George. Let me know what I can do to help."

The third message was from Mark, President and CEO of the company, as well as the husband of my best friend Nancy. "Amy," he said, "George tells me we've had a bad fire. Possibly a total loss, from what he says. You and I need to discuss this tomorrow. Please come to my office the first thing in the morning."

That was Mark the CEO talking, not Mark my best friend Nancy's husband. I liked the second guy better. And damn that George, blowing the fire way out of proportion like that. Had to tattle on me without having even half the facts. I wasn't worried about Mark, though. He was a reasonable guy. Once he'd heard me out, he'd realize that George was a total donkey, if he didn't know that already.

I filled Pete in on the latest as we enjoyed our champagne. "One thing's evident. Life is never dull at NEC&I." I snuggled up to him on the couch.

"So it seems. Sometimes I wonder how you put up with it as well as you do."

"It's definitely not because of the big bucks they pay me. Sometimes I do wish for a calmer work environment. That will probably never happen. At least the job is seldom boring. It's at times like this that I love having Sam around. He's such a good listener. Spilling my guts to him always helps me keep things in perspective."

"I'm a pretty good listener too, you know." Pete graced me with an impish grin.

"True, most of the time. But Sam never asks questions or talks back or contradicts me. He is such a great best friend."

Pete gave me an odd look." I thought I was your best friend."

"Of course you are," I said. "You and Sam both." *And Nancy.*

"That's a relief. How can I help you at the moment?"

"By keeping my mind off tomorrow and what may happen when I get to the office. Something tells me it may not be pretty."

CHAPTER 10

I was up before the sun the next morning, relaxed, well-rested and eager to pick up my pal Sam at the veterinary clinic. Pete took off early, heading home to change into a business suit, then to meet with a new client. We'd get together for dinner to compare days. We'd been doing that a lot lately. It was nice. Sharing with Sam was one thing; Pete brought it to a whole new level.

I beat the morning traffic heading through Boston, which was a nice surprise. Having Henry greet me at the door of the clinic was surprising as well. I thought he had an overnight assistant.

"Good morning, Amy. How are you today?"

"I'm fine. More importantly, how is Sam?" I said a quick prayer that my best buddy had made it through his ordeal unscathed.

"Poor guy had a rather miserable night, but he's doing fine now. Let me get him for you."

I let out the breath I didn't realize I'd been holding.

Sam bounded out of the back room, overjoyed at the sight of me. It's nice to be missed. Now I could have two delightful reunions, one with Sam and one with Henry.

"I didn't expect to see you here this early," I said. "Did your overnight assistant quit?"

"Nope. I gave her the night off so I could be with my favorite patient." Henry smiled down at Sam. "It's good to see you, too, Amy. I keep meaning to call you about getting together to catch up, then…"

"I know. Life gets in the way." And all too often we just sit back and let that happen. "So, my buddy is going to be all right?"

"Better than all right," he told me. "Good old Sam is good as new. And apparently still up to his old tricks, eating off the sidewalk like that. A bad habit. It's going to catch up with him one of these days. We don't want that to happen."

Was that Henry's subtle way of scolding me? I was trying with Sam. Truly I was. "We're working on it, believe me. I don't want anything to happen to my buddy."

"Speaking of friends, I spoke with Danny's parents last week," he told me. "They said they'd seen you recently."

"Right, in October. Pete and I spent a long weekend in Montréal. I gave them a call."

"Wasn't that awkward – your deceased fiancé's parents and your new boyfriend?"

"Believe it or not, it was Pete's idea. He thought I'd find it easier to move on with my life if I knew I had Danny's family's approval. He may have been right. The four of us had a lovely dinner at Les Halles."

Henry smiled. "I know the place well. Incredible food. Just the thought of it makes me hungry. It was always one of Danny's favorite places."

A dark cloud passed over his face. I knew the feeling all too well.

"Dan's parents told me how much they liked Pete. They're pleased to see you happy."

"They're good people. Listen, I have to get going. I'm already late for work. But let's make it a point to get together soon." I paid the bill and led Sam to the car. "OK, Buddy, let's get you home so I can get to work. I have a feeling it's going to be a long, unpleasant day." I scratched his head; he wagged his tail. My cell phone rang.

Jimmy Landry the arson investigator.

"Good morning, Jimmy." I left the car in park and put the phone on speaker. "Please tell me you have some news for me." I searched through my bag as I spoke, fishing out a notebook and pen. "Have you determined what started the fire?"

"I believe so, though neither the reason nor the motive. It may have been either arson or an accident, and an interesting accident at that. We're just not sure."

"You're talking in circles, Jimmy. Let's start over. What started the fire?"

"Looks like it was marijuana."

"Say that again?"

"Marijuana. Weed. Mary Jane."

Hmmmm. One of the fencers said that Howie Zupkoff had been acting strangely. Maybe he was high. Did he start the fire? "What makes you think that?" I asked.

"We found a packet of rolling papers, on the floor in the undamaged area of the cellar. It was crisp and new. Obviously hadn't been there long. It was lying in an area jam-packed with oily rags, cardboard boxes, old newspapers and other such flammable junk. Turpentine, for one thing. Not to mention a metal box filled with exceptionally large bullets. Also, whoever was down there had to have come from inside the house. I'm guessing it was one of the tenants down there chilling out who started it all."

"Why do you say that?"

"Nobody could have entered through the bulkhead. From the looks of it, it had been nailed shut from the inside for years. That is, until the police took a hatchet to it yesterday so they could get the body out. And the lock on the inside door was rusted closed. The property owner was here earlier installing a whole new door."

"I'm sorry to say there is one small problem with that theory," I told Jimmy. "The owner, informed me yesterday that the front door lock was broken. That means that anybody off the street could have entered the building. The question then becomes, once inside, could a person get down into the cellar easily?"

"I can answer that," Jimmy said. "The door to the cellar stairs is off the first floor hallway. It doesn't have a lock. That expands our list of possible suspects to the public at large."

"Bummer." I groaned as I gave this some additional thought.

"That's for sure," Jimmy said. "The best we can come up with is that whoever was down there flicked some ashes and also knocked over a can of turpentine."

I tried to envision this scenario. It seemed a bit of a stretch. "Sounds like a very clumsy person, don't you think?" *Or a very high one.*

"Or somebody doing these things deliberately," Jimmy said. "Accident or not, the basic sequence of events remains the same."

I thought this over. "Maybe something spooked the person smoking the joint, setting off the rest of it." *Like maybe spotting a dead fencer on the floor?*

"Could be," Jimmy said. "At any rate, live ashes made contact with turpentine. We may never know exactly how or why. What we do know is that some combustibles were ignited. Then the fire grew fairly quickly. As it heated up, it also ignited a few stray bullets lying on the floor. If it had lit up the entire box a few feet away, there would have been one heck of an explosion. When the fire got going, the unknown smoker must have dropped the joint not far from the stairway and run."

That sounded reasonable enough. Odd, but feasible. "The question now becomes: did our perp run because the fire started, because the ammunition was about to explode or because he or she spotted the body or perhaps even the killer?" I asked.

"Or maybe he was the killer. But unless we catch this perp, we may never know the answer to any of that."

"One can always hope."

"But that's not actually why I phoned you," Jimmy said. "And this is where the plot begins to thicken, or at least to take a few nasty, circuitous turns."

"That sounds ominous. What is it?"

"This part is actually beyond my job description. Once the cause of the fire is determined, I'm technically done. The police are in charge from that time on. But I know you, and like you. I thought you might be interested in what else was found here today. I don't know if it'll help your case or not."

"What is it?"

"Well, as I said before, the cellar floor is packed dirt. That was a lucky break for us."

"Because …?"

"It has track marks on it, the kind you'd get from dragging a body across the area. We followed the trail from where the body was found to the opposite end of the cellar. There was a smattering of blood along the way as well, so we're positive the body was moved."

"Why would anybody do that?"

"Unknown at this time. But at the end of the drag marks, or the beginning actually, we found what appears to be the murder weapon."

Now we were getting somewhere.

Jimmy was really dragging this out. And I was beginning to lose my patience. "What was it?"

"A pick mattock."

Now he had my full attention. "What the hell is a pick mattock?"

"It's a common gardening tool, used to break up hard-packed soil. You can buy one in any gardening shop or hardware store. It has a long wooden handle. The end has a metal shovel-like head similar to an axe blade on one side and an adze, or pick axe, which is pretty sharp, on the other. All in all, it's the perfect choice of a tool to loosen a packed-dirt cellar floor."

"Not to mention committing murder. Did the police get any fingerprints off it?"

"Unfortunately not. The damn tool had been wiped clean. But they were able to retrieve a trace of blood."

"So they can test it for DNA?" I asked.

"It's possible. But that decision needs to be authorized by the detective in charge."

"Why do they need to authorize DNA tests?"

"These tests are time-consuming and expensive. Only to be done when absolutely necessary," Jimmy told me.

This case was getting more interesting by the minute. I checked my watch and considered my options, then asked him, "Are you still at the property?"

"Yes I am. Why?"

"I'm just a few blocks away. At the veterinarian's on Freeport Street. How about my dog and I join you over there? I'd love to see this for myself."

"That's actually the reason for my call."

"What do you mean?"

"All of this information was just backdrop, or build-up."

"Backdrop for what?"

"I think I'd rather tell you the rest in person."

"I'll be right there." I scratched behind Sam's ears and put the Mustang in gear, wondering what I'd done to deserve so much additional information from Jimmy. And hoping his help didn't come with strings attached.

CHAPTER 11

Sam and I arrived at the house on Chadwick Street five minutes later. The crime scene van was parked outside, the yellow police tape still in place. Andy was standing on the front steps looking lost and helpless.

"Where's the arson investigator?" I asked him.

"In the cellar. He said for us to wait here until he comes back out."

"Did he say anything about what's going on?"

Andy shook his head. "Not to me. I'm waiting for the building inspector. The police told me he can't go into the cellar yet, but he can check out the rest of the building. They said if he declares the place safe, it's OK for you or an appraiser to go in as well. Just stay away from the cellar for now. I hope the arson investigator gets here soon. I need to get his OK so Freddy and his team can pick up their belongings and get back to school."

I struggled to put my curiosity on hold, got Sam out of the car and sat on the front steps with Andy. "Those poor kids must be going stir crazy camping out at the fencing club," I said. "This trip has been tough on them."

"That's for sure," Andy said. "They're meeting with a grief counsellor this morning. That was Pete's doing. And a great idea. Then, after I deal with the building inspector, Freddy and I are taking the team on a sight-seeing tour of Boston, hoping we can cheer them up a little, or at least distract them for a while. We'll do the Museum of Science, the Freedom Trail, maybe a Duck Boat ride. Anything to keep them busy, and keep their minds off Howie and Bob. Pete plans to join us if he can get away."

Hmmm. Pete was spending the afternoon out of the office? Again. He'd been doing that a lot lately. What was going on with him? I knew he was unhappy at his job and wanted to make a change, but if he kept up this type of behavior, maybe his departure wouldn't be voluntary. That was a worry.

"You're a nice guy, Andy," I told him.

He smiled. "I try."

I did a quick inspection of the work Andy and Pete had done boarding things up. Looked good to me. "Nice job on the door and windows," I told Andy.

He gave me a thin smile. "Couldn't have done it without Pete."

That took me aback. My experience with Pete had always been that he was all thumbs.

Two vehicles screeched to a halt in front of us, a police car and the medical examiner's van. Detective Donnelly from the meeting at the fencing club, a second cop and a man from the medical examiner's office dashed around behind the house without acknowledging me or Andy. A few moments later, the arson investigator joined us on the front steps.

"Jimmy," I said to him, "what's going on here? Has something else happened?"

He let out a ragged breath. "As I was telling you on the phone, the police found a trail of blood in the dirt of the cellar floor."

"Right. And ...?"

"They followed the trail back to where the body had originally fallen, clear on the other end of the cellar."

"And …?"

"Somebody had been digging there. Recently. And was apparently scared off before he finished. The cops dug further down and uncovered a grimy old suitcase with a rusted metal closure. It had to be pried open." He hung his head.

"Jimmy, what is it? What was in the suitcase?" I was almost afraid to know.

He choked back a sob. "Under a small pile of yellowed newspapers and what was left of a tattered blue blanket, they found the skeletal remains of a child. A very small child."

I didn't know whether to cry or throw up. "Oh my God! I can't believe all this is happening. It's too awful for words."

Jimmy shook his head. "I know. It looks like the poor baby has been here for quite a while. The newspaper was from 1998. Yes, it has been quite a while indeed."

Andy reached over and brushed a tear from my cheek. "Two bodies in two days in the same damn cellar. Can it get any worse than this? It's just too grim." He put his head in his hands and sobbed. "This can't be happening."

I gave him a hug. We both cried a little. Then, as if on cue, both of us pulled ourselves together. Sort of.

"Take a deep breath, Amy," Jimmy said. "You're looking a bit shaky."

"I'll be fine," I told him, willing it to be so. Then I changed the subject, hoping that talking business would keep me from falling apart. "I am curious about something."

"What's that?"

"I'm grateful you shared this plethora of dreadful information with me. You didn't have to do that. Why did you?"

He gave me a killer smile. "I like you, Amy. You know that. I thought you might find some of this helpful." He hesitated and stared at the ground. "Besides, I thought I might convince you to join me for dinner sometime."

That was not what I wanted to hear.

Before I came up with an appropriately kind response, Jimmy shook his head and added, "Or not." He headed back toward the rear of the house, then turned and added, "I would've told you anyway."

I left Sam with Andy and walked to the sidewalk, where I summoned every ounce of strength that I could and called Peggy.

"Where are you, Amy? I've been worried. People have been looking for you. Unhappy people. Is everything all right?"

"Nothing's all right at the moment. I'll fill you in when I see you. I just can't talk about it right now." I fought back tears.

"If you say so. In the meantime, what shall I tell Mark and George, as well as the entire Underwriting Department?"

"Tell them that we've got a situation on Chadwick Street. A bad one. The police and the medical examiner are here and I need to remain at the scene to answer their questions. That ought to give everybody something to wonder about."

"Geez, Amy. None of that sounds good. But you don't have to talk about it now if you don't want to. I'll keep myself occupied thinking up all sorts of horrible possible scenarios. In the meantime, what can I do to help?"

"Can you hold down the fort for a while longer?"

"Always. Any idea when I might see your sad old face again?"

"My best guess is tomorrow. There's no telling how long I'll be here. Can you fend off the angry mob until then?"

CHAPTER 12

The building inspector had arrived while I was speaking with Peggy. He and Andy were conferring with one of the crime scene techs on the sidewalk. Detective Donnelly, wearing a rumpled gray suit, joined them. "I can't let you into the cellar yet," he said to the inspector. "Not until the crime scene folks and the medical examiner are finished."

"Any idea how long that will be?" the inspector asked.

Donnelly shrugged. "In the meantime, there's no reason you can't take a look at the rest of the building."

"Shall I go with you?" Andy asked.

The inspector shook his head. "No need." And off he went.

Andy looked like he was about to collapse. I patted his hand, then relieved him of Sam's leash. "I know how upsetting this mess is for you, particularly this latest development. We will sort it all out in time. In the meantime, you need to think of Freddy and his fencers. There's no point in letting them know anything about the latest development. And you did promise them a fun day sightseeing in Boston. Do you think you can hold it together for a while longer?" *Please say yes.*

"Will do" Andy said. "Thanks for being here for me, Amy."

Pete's car pulled up in front of the house. Sam and I rushed over and gave him an abbreviated update. He looked horror stricken. "Holy shit! What can I do to help?"

"Take Andy with you. Tour the city with Freddy and the team. Distract them all as best you can. But don't tell them about what's been happening. And keep Andy calm. He's nearly at the breaking point."

Pete gave me a quick kiss on the forehead. "Your wish is my command. Can we talk about this in detail over dinner?"

I doubted I'd have much appetite after a day like this, but time with Pete was time with Pete. And I needed that right now. "Absolutely. Call me later."

Donnelly stood in the yard watching me. "Ms. Lynch," he growled, "Long time no see."

I shrugged. "What can I say, Detective? We've got to stop meeting like this."

"Trouble sure seems to follow you around." He shook his head. "Remind me never to get on your bad side."

"Duly noted."

I steeled myself as best I could before asking Donnelly the question that was on my mind. I'd be damned if I'd let the man see any sign of the weakness I was feeling. "Would it be all right if Andy took off for a couple of hours? It's really important. And he doesn't know anything anyway."

Donnelly glared at me.

"Please," I pleaded.

"Oh, all right. I guess so. We can question you at length later, Mr. Yesley. Come by the station at 5:00."

Donnelly frowned at me. "You do realize you're not in charge here, right?"

I bit my tongue, not wanting to piss him off. Staying on his good side could only help my investigation. I hoped I was already there, albeit on somewhat shaky ground.

He finally noticed Sam. "This your dog?"

I nodded. Sam wagged his tail and grinned up at Donnelly.

"What's he doing here?"

"He was with me when I got the call from Jimmy Landry."

"He was going to work with you?" Donnelly asked, looking at my navy pin-striped business suit. "Does he do that often?"

"Sometimes," I said. "He's very well behaved." I probably should have explained about Sam's night at the vet. Oh well, if Donnelly wanted to know more, he'd ask. And I'd tell him. "Don't worry, Detective. Sam hasn't been inside the building."

Donnelly frowned. "I think you better put him in your car. Just to be sure. Can't risk having him get loose and go messing up my crime scene any more than it already has been. And please remember, your interest here is in the damage to the building. And that's all."

"Maybe not," I said, trying not to sound too sassy. "We also provide liability coverage on this property. You never know what people might come up with in an effort to blame Andy for their troubles. And file a suit against him. I have to gather all the facts to document my file. My company needs to be prepared, just in case." I was stretching things here, but it was a vague possibility. Donnelly seemed to accept it.

"You sure like to be in the thick of things, don't you, Ms. Lynch?" He turned and headed back to the rear of the house.

I called to him, "Before you leave, please tell me I can go into the building and do a quick look-around. It would help me get my investigation moving. I promise I'll stay away from the cellar."

"Yeah" he mumbled. "Go ahead."

I had the urge to salute the man, but thought better of it. There was no sense annoying him any more than I already had. This was a sad and serious business. I shouldn't be flip about it, even if it did help me to cope.

I put Sam in the car then walked toward the building, bracing myself against the stench of old smoke. I'd get an appraiser out as fast as I could to determine repair and clean-up costs. All I needed today was a general idea of what we were dealing with.

Things were pretty much as I had been told. The apartment on the first floor left was in bad shape. The walls were badly burned, as were the floors. Everything would need to be replaced. A few windows were blown out as well. They were boarded up for the moment until Andy could replace them. While Andy was working on the walls and floors, he should probably update the kitchen and bathroom as well. They certainly needed it. He probably couldn't afford it, though. And that type of work, actually renovation, wouldn't be covered by insurance.

The rest of the building had smoke damage – dirty, smelly and not too costly to handle. If I were the woman in the other first floor apartment, I'd get rid of all the furniture. It stunk. Andy said she was staying at her daughter's. Maybe she wouldn't need the furniture anymore.

The two second floor units were vacant and unfurnished. Both were cluttered with the fencers' sleeping bags and assorted belongings. Both apartments on the third floor were occupied. Also messy, in serious need of updates and reeking of smoke. NEC&I would pay for ServPro to mitigate the smoke damage. The rest was up to Andy.

Back outside, I retrieved Sam from the car in case he needed a pit stop.

The fellow I assumed was the medical examiner came around from out back. Not the same person as yesterday. This was an older man, with a shock of thick white hair and what looked to be a tailor-made suit. Nicely polished shoes, too. And leather gloves.

"Amy Lynch, from New England Casualty and Indemnity." I said as I handed him my card.

"Ted Rosen, Chief Medical Examiner." he said as he shook my hand. He looked down at Sam. "And who is this??"

"My dog Sam."

"Please tell me he hasn't been anywhere near the crime scene."

I shook my head. "Never left the front yard."

"Be sure to keep it that way." Rosen bent down and patted Sam on the head. "Good boy." He turned to me. "What kind of dog is he?"

"Border collie beagle mix."

"That explains why he looks so bright and alert. Border collies are one of the most intelligent breeds, you know." He patted Sam again.

I knew what he meant. Sam and I had wonderful chats together, though I usually did most of the talking. Right now my pal was in hog heaven with all this attention.

Rosen gazed at the official vehicles parked in front of the house. "From what I've been told, it looks like the crime scene folks might be here for a while yet."

I sensed a possible opportunity here and decided to go for it even though I knew what the outcome would probably be. "May I ask you something, just out of curiosity?"

Rosen raised his eyebrows. "What's that?"

"It's about the body they found is in an old suitcase. Will someone check the suitcase for fingerprints?"

"Of course, that's standard operating procedure."

"When the results come in, who gets the report?"

"The police."

"Anybody else?"

"Not usually. Why?"

"Just thought I'd ask." I hesitated, then added, "Is it the same story with DNA?"

"Right."

"I see." I wracked my brains looking for some way to get a copy of the results. Nothing occurred to me.

He gave me a curious look. "Excuse me for bringing this up, but isn't your job here to deal with the fire loss?"

"Correct," I said.

"And you're not connected with the police in any way?"

I shook my head.

"Then why all these questions? Your company doesn't have a vested interest in the bodies discovered here."

"Detective Donnelly said the same thing. And you're both mistaken. My gut tells me it's all connected somehow. The fire, the dead fencer and the baby. And figuring out one of these questions may just solve them all. For the police and for NEC&I."

He frowned again. "Interesting theory. And for all I know, you may be right. You seem like a nice person. I wish you luck."

"Thanks." I flashed him what I hoped was my sweetest, most sincere smile.

Detective Donnelly joined us and made a big noisy deal about clearing his throat.

We jumped to attention.

"OK," he announced, "Here's the deal. Nobody says a word about this second body until we have a better grasp of what's going on. We've got officers canvassing the neighborhood. Maybe one of them will learn something that will help us sort this out. For now, we're not releasing any of this information to the press. Let's keep things quiet for as long as we can."

"There may be one small problem with that," I told him.

"And that would be …?"

"The neighbors, particularly the lady next door."

"What about her?" Donnelly barked.

"She's very interested in what's going on in her neighborhood. And I'm pretty sure she has noticed the medical examiner's van by now. She'll know that something's up."

Donnelly frowned and rubbed his chin. "Can you come up with some kind of story? Anything that'll keep her quiet for the moment. Like perhaps we were all back here to look for additional evidence, or something like that?"

"I'll do my best." *And then you'll owe me a favor. Not a bad deal.*

"And, Detective, I'm assuming it will be all right for my appraiser to inspect the building tomorrow."

Donnelly scowled, then grumbled. "Yeah. OK. But make very sure he stays away from the cellar. And after that nobody else gets inside until and unless I say so."

"Thanks. I will personally supervise his inspection. You can count on me." I hoped I'd be able to count on Detective Donnelly as well. For what, I wasn't sure yet. But there was bound to be something.

CHAPTER 13

I remained on the sidewalk watching as the baby's remains were loaded into the medical examiner's vehicle, trying to process the morning's events. Not an easy task. I also needed to decide what my next move should be. Sitting on the front porch had left my clothes smelling like smoke. I had to change them. I didn't want to go to the office and face Mark like this. George sure, but not my boss. I walked toward my Mustang.

Mrs. Czwakiel called to me as she headed down her front stairs. "Hello, Amy. Please tell me it's all right to call you Amy."

The woman was all bundled up in her winter coat, scarf and gloves. No more fuzzy pink slippers. Either she was on her way somewhere or she planned to be outside for a while.

"Of course it's all right." She never gave me the option of using her Helen. At least I thought that was the name I had heard.

"And who is this handsome creature?"

"My dog. Sam, say hello to Mrs. Czwakiel."

Sam sat and offered her his paw.

"Well, how do you do Sam? It's very nice to meet you." She bent down to shake hands with him. "Amy, I'm not sure I really want to know, but please tell me anyway, how is the investigation going?"

I was afraid to tell her anything. "It's difficult to say. These things take time, you know."

"I'm sure they do. I couldn't help but notice, though, that the police and the medical examiner are back. And they've been here for a while now. What's that all about?"

I gazed down at Sam and answered, "Oh, you know, just looking to collect additional evidence. They don't want to move too fast and miss something important."

She gave me a look that was reminiscent of my third grade teacher when I gave her a lame excuse for not having done my homework. "I'm sure that's true. However, I wasn't born yesterday. If the police are back here, I know that something is up. And I saw what they brought out just now. Even without my glasses, it sure looked to me like a small body bag, the kind you might use for a child."

The woman obviously watched a lot of TV. I tried to play dumb. "A body bag?"

It didn't work.

She gave me an all-knowing look. "Yes. A body bag. What do you know about it?"

"Sorry, Mrs. Czwakiel. I really can't say."

"I suppose you can't," she said. "I understand. Mum's the word. Anyway, I might be mistaken. I hope I am. Besides, I can't remember the last time there were children in that house."

Based on the newspapers in the suitcase it would have been twenty years ago. Mrs. Czwakiel lived in the neighborhood at the time. Should I begin to question her memory? Or perhaps pick her brain for more info?

She pursed her lips. "I'll ask Beatrice if she remembers anybody with a baby living here. Though I've got to say, her memory isn't quite what it used to be."

Happens to the best of us. "That'd be helpful. Thanks."

"I have something to tell you," she said. "Something that happened last night."

I gave her my full attention. "What was that?"

"Well, I was up in the night. When you get to be my age, you don't sleep so well. I usually get up and walk around a bit, maybe make a nice cup of chamomile tea. As I said, I was awake. It was about two in the morning. And I heard something next door. Behind the house. Like someone was trying to get in through the back door. I turned on my light and called out, 'Who's there?' but nobody answered. Then I believe I saw someone running through the back yard. What do you think about that?"

"Did you call the police?"

"Of course, but by the time they arrived, whoever had been there was long gone."

"Can you describe him?"

"Not really. It was too dark. And I couldn't remember where I'd left my glasses. Do you think it might be connected to the fire and… and… and to the rest of it?" she asked.

"That's very possible." Time to change the subject. "Are you on your way someplace?"

Before she could answer, two men called out to her from the house across the street. Good looking guys, fashionably dressed, maybe in their late twenties. They were both tall, one dark, one fair, with a greyhound on a leash. "Hello, Mrs. C. How are you today?"

She squinted in their direction. "Oh, hello boys," she called to them. "Come over here and meet Amy Lynch." She whispered to me, "Don't set your sights on either of them. They're gay. Not that there's anything wrong with that. It's just the way God made them."

The two men joined us on the sidewalk.

"Hello Amy Lynch," one of them said. "It's nice to meet you. I'm James Eck. This is my partner Ryan Izbicki." He looked down at the greyhound. "And this beautiful canine is Fifi."

"She looks like she wants to meet your dog," Ryan said.

We handled the introductions. Sam and Fifi wagged their respective tails and went through the usual canine greeting rituals.

I looked at their property across the street. Nice-looking house. A pale yellow exterior with blue and white trim, it reminded me of the painted ladies of San Francisco. "You guys have a lovely home."

"Thanks," James said. "We just repainted it. We're also redecorating the inside, one room at a time. Furnishing it with lots and lots of fabulous antiques. Mostly from England. We go there once a year on antiquing expeditions. It's wonderful fun. You must stop by and see the house when we have more time."

"I'd like that."

"Amy is an investigator," Mrs. Czwakiel told them. "From the insurance company. She's trying to figure out what's been going on over here in number twelve. But don't ask her too much about it just now. She's sworn to secrecy until the authorities know more."

That was an interesting take on the conversation she and I just had. I decided I better not try to put anything over on the woman.

She pointed to Andy's house. "It's all so upsetting what happened in there, don't you boys agree?"

"That's for sure," James said. "There hasn't been much good happening in that house for ages. Bad things going on. Bad people doing them."

Mrs. Czwakiel said, "Tell us about it, please. We're all ears. I'm sure anything you know will help Amy's investigation."

"It's that damn guy, what's his name?" James turned to Ryan.

"Charlie Florescu," Ryan responded. "Not Charles, mind you, like any self-respecting fellow. No, this one is just plain Charlie. He's the BFF of Ellen who lives on the third floor, and a real piece of work. He's a total creep if you ask me. Always lurking around here looking like he's up to no good, which I'm sure is the case." He rolled his pale blue eyes.

I pulled out my notebook and pen. "Charlie Florescu, huh? What do you know about him?"

"Not much actually," James said. "Ellen introduced him to us once, when she first moved in here. He was rude from the get-go. Simply no manners at all."

"And he treats Ellen like dirt," Ryan added. "Always yelling at her, calling her a useless whore. Excuse my language. Just quoting, you know. I figured that he's her pimp."

"And a drug dealer," James piped in. "I've seen him selling, right out on the sidewalk. Even in the middle of the day."

Ryan chimed in. "Not only that, but the guy hates dogs. I could just tell, the way he always looked at Fifi. How can anybody not love such an adorable creature?"

"Fifi does growl at him a lot," James said, "but that's no reason to hate her. She's a dog. That's what they do. And he teases her when she's outside. She has a doggie door to her fenced-in yard, so she's outside a lot. That man comes by and taunts her. He is just plain mean. It's as if he's deliberately trying to upset our girl. Can you believe that?"

What I could believe was that I'd like to learn a lot more about Charlie Florescu. The sooner the better.

Detective Donnelly emerged from the cellar and signaled for me to join them. I said good-bye to Mrs. Czwakiel and my new friends, then obeyed orders. "What's up, Detective?"

"I just spoke with the building inspector. He says this property is structurally sound."

"Does that mean Andy can have ServPro come in and begin the clean-up?"

"Yes indeed. But, as I've said before, only from the ground floor up. The cellar is still an active crime scene. That also means we don't want the tenants moving back in yet."

"What about the fencing team?" I asked. "Is it all right if they come by to retrieve their belongings?"

Donnelly gave this some thought. "I guess there's no reason why not. But they'd have to do so under strict police supervision of course. I'll speak with their coach and make the arrangements."

"If you arrange for them to come by tomorrow morning, I can plan to be here as well. I'd be happy to help. And I would like to see the kids again before they head home."

"You certainly don't want to miss anything, do you?" He sighed. "I suppose it would be all right for you to be here, as long as you don't interfere."

That was a step in the right direction. Maybe I was growing on the man.

"Just one more thing," he added.

"What's that?"

"Tomorrow, don't bring your dog."

By the time Donnelly left, it was mid-afternoon. I was debating whether or not to bother going to the office when I spotted Andy's tenant Douglas Weiss approaching the house.

"Good afternoon." He smiled at me. "Ms. Lynch, isn't it?"

"Mr. Weiss. What brings you here today?"

He looked at the house and frowned. "Just checking on things. I was hoping the crime scene tape would be down by now and I could get into my apartment to pick up a few things."

"Sorry. The authorities aren't quite finished." I wasn't about to offer him any additional info, not wanting to upset my new friend Detective Donnelly.

"I was also hoping to catch the mailman, or at least see if he left anything for me"

"I haven't seen the mailman," I told him. "And I have no idea how mail delivery is handled, or not, in a situation like this. Sorry I can't be more helpful."

"Not your fault. Guess I'll just be on my way then." He gave me a small smile and walked away.

I decided it was too late in the day to accomplish much at the office. I convinced myself I should just bring Sam home and change my clothes for dinner with Pete. I knew I was being a coward, and didn't really care. I'd deal with George, Mark and the rest of them in the morning.

CHAPTER 14

Sam was happy to be back on his own turf. He followed me around the apartment with a love-sick puppy expression on his face. I gave him the abbreviated version of what had been going on at the office. Also thanked him for being with me on Chadwick Street. Just having him nearby somehow helped to keep me calm and in control. "And you made a new friend, didn't you?"

He wagged his whole body.

I made a quick call to Andy.

"What's up, Amy? And please tell me it's good news."

"You'll be happy to know that your building is structurally sound. We can contact ServPro to start working on the clean-up. That'll get rid of the odor of smoke."

"Who's ServPro? Or perhaps what?"

"It's a fire restoration company. We use them a lot. Their motto says that they make things 'like it never even happened.'"

"Let's hope they're right about that," he said.

"And they can bill NEC&I directly."

"That's great. I'm a little strapped for cash right now."

"Also, the police said that Freddy and his team can pick up their gear at your place tomorrow morning. Detective Donnelly will be contacting Freddy to make arrangements. I plan to be there as well."

"That's great. The team will be delighted. I know how anxious they are to head home."

"I'm sure. See you later."

Pete picked me up around 6:00. We made a pact not to dwell on the day's unpleasantness then headed for Dali's on the Cambridge-Somerville line, one of my favorite local restaurants. It had a funky, casual atmosphere, a delicious assortment of tapas and some truly outstanding sangria.

We selected six tapas, which we would share. Braised rabbit, roast duck, garlic shrimp, skewers with ham, cheese and melon, stuffed mushrooms and mussels in white wine. And of course a large pitcher of sangria. We tried to unwind as we compared notes on our days.

"How are Freddy's fencers doing? Did they enjoy Boston?" I asked.

"Yes, I believe they did. The distraction was good for them. And, despite the cold, at least the sun was out."

"What did they like best?"

Pete gave that a bit of thought. "Two things, actually. They loved the Duck Boat Tour, particularly the part where we were cruising on the Charles River. Andy and I entertained them with our version of 'Love that Dirty Water.' The kids thought we were a hoot."

"I wish I'd been there for that." I didn't know about Andy, but Pete was not particularly known for his singing abilities. "What else did they like?"

"The Museum of Science. And it was so convenient that the Duck Tour began and ended there, since the place has a large indoor parking garage. It eliminated what could have turned into a logistical nightmare looking for a place to put two vans."

"I figured they would love the museum. Most of the fencers I've known seem to have a degree in some technical scientific field of study."

"That's fencing for you," Pete told me. "It attracts the brainy type. Think of it as chess with a weapon."

Our sangria arrived. We filled our glasses and toasted each other.

"Andy called a while ago," he said. "He told me the fencers are picking up their gear tomorrow. That's great news. They're all getting antsy camping out at the fencing club. Particularly Freddy. He feels responsible for the whole darn mess. And he's a wreck worrying that Howie's parents will try to hold him responsible for their son's death, though, legally speaking, I can't come up with a scenario that would make that work."

"I think he's feeling responsible for everything these days," I said. *As was Andy. Both of them seemed a little shaky.*

"Agreed. Have you recovered from your day?" he asked.

I knew we were slipping into a conversation we had decided not to have, but I couldn't help it. Pete was a wonderful listener, almost as good as Sam.

"I'm all right. Or at least I will be. I cannot, will not, let it get to me. On the other hand, it is unsettling that we've found two bodies in that cellar. I just know they're all somehow connected. What do you think?"

"I think you've got an over-active imagination, but one never knows."

"You are aware that there's no such thing as a coincidence?"

Pete grinned at me. "I've heard that said. Not sure I believe it."

"I bet you dinner at a five-star restaurant that they are connected."

He laughed. "You're on. And I get to pick the place. It will be interesting to see how all this plays out. Let's just hope there aren't any more bodies down there. I don't think Andy could deal with that."

"Agreed. Poor guy needs a break. " I drained my glass and refilled it, right to the top.

"Are the police making any progress on Howie Zupkoff's death?" he asked.

"Not that I've heard. I'm learning more from the neighbors on Chadwick Street than from the cops." I gave him the low-down on Mrs. Czwakiel, James and Ryan across the street and Fifi the greyhound. "It's an interesting neighborhood."

"Sure sounds it. What do you think about that Florescu guy? Does he look like a good suspect for anything nefarious?" Pete asked.

"My gut tells me he's got to be guilty of something connected to that house. Only time will tell what, and whether or not it's related to my case."

Our tapas arrived, piping hot and smelling wonderful. We spent a few minutes filling our plates. Then something occurred to me. I didn't want to spoil our evening, but I did need to know what was going on with Pete. "Did you have any trouble getting the afternoon off to join Andy and the fencing team?"

"Actually, I didn't ask. Just went."

I wondered if this would be a problem for him tomorrow. He didn't seem worried about it. I forced myself to let it go. "You were still in your lawyer suit when you arrived at Chadwick Street today. So you did work this morning?"

"Worked, yes, but not at the office."

"Explain yourself." I smiled as I said this, so as not to appear as bossy as I sounded.

"We have a new client," he began. "A middle-aged woman who is confined to a wheel-chair. It's difficult for her to get around, particularly coming into the city. I took the train out to meet with her at her home."

That was my Pete. Always happy to help somebody out. Also always happy to spend time away from his stress-filled office. "Where does she live?"

"Massapoag Junction."

"You're making that name up, right? I've never heard of such a town. "

"Nope," he grinned. "It's a real town, or a village actually."

"With a name like that, it must be somewhere in the back of beyond."

"Believe it or not, it's only a short train ride from Boston. Nestled between Easton and Sharon."

"At least I've heard of those towns. What's this Junction like?"

"Massapoag Junction, Amy. Get it right."

Pete was nothing if not precise, which was probably what made him a good lawyer. I remembered something from a claim I had investigated in Sharon a while ago. "Is that where Lake Massapoag is?"

"Actually no. The lake is in Sharon. But Massapoag Junction has some really picturesque little ponds. Several that I saw. My client lives on one of them."

"Please tell me more."

It's a pretty nice place. Smaller than either Easton or Sharon. It has a lot of charm, a lot of quaint old houses. And a population around nine thousand. There's a small downtown area with a post office, a coffee shop, a couple of restaurants and an apothecary."

"You mean a drugstore."

"Maybe," he said. "The sign says apothecary. There's also a train station within walking distance of the center."

"Sounds like you checked this place out in detail. How come?" I thought I knew the answer, but better to let him say it.

"I'm thinking it might be exactly the type of town I've been hoping to find. Someplace small and friendly, out of the city but not too far. I might just want to move there one of these days. And sooner rather than later."

That wasn't a surprise. Pete had been talking about making a change for a while now. He wanted to escape the rat-race of Boston and become a small town lawyer. "Are you telling me you've given your notice at work?"

He shook his head. "Not yet. I want to wait until I have some firm plans - a small house with a big yard and a mortgage that won't break my budget. Hopefully on a pond. And not too far away from you."

"It sounds like you may have just found the town."

"Maybe. Now I just need to find the right house."

I hoped he would. And soon. I wanted him to be happy. And I'd find a way to deal with whatever he ended up doing.

CHAPTER 15

I was hoping to sneak into my office early Wednesday morning to attack some paperwork without having to speak with anyone. No such luck. George was waiting at my door with his arms crossed and a smug look on his face. I hated that look. He and I had always had issues, mostly because he had a nasty disposition and a maliciously competitive nature. When I got promoted over him a few years ago, he had waged all-out war on me. He was forever trying to catch me being anything less than perfect.

"So, Hotshot," he sneered. "How's your week going? Haven't seen much of you. Where have you been keeping yourself?"

I willed myself to smile at the man. It was either smile or slap his face. "Just doing my job. Out collecting evidence, assessing damage. You know how it goes."

"Must have been a lot of evidence if it took you two entire days. Did it have anything to do with that terrible fire?"

I walked past him to my desk. I didn't offer him a seat.

"I heard it was a big fire."

I ignored him and removed my coat.

"Isn't this the property you begged Underwriting to accept as a special favor to you?"

"Right." *What of it? Sometimes we do each other favors in this business.* "Did you need me for anything in particular? Something beyond your authority perhaps?" I couldn't resist goading him.

He continued as if he hadn't heard me. "Wasn't this the property which is only fifty percent occupied? The one we knew was in less-than-desirable condition? The one with a laundry list of adverse loss history?"

"Any prior losses happened long before Andy bought the place. Long before we insured it." I sat down and booted up my computer hoping he'd take the hint and leave.

He didn't.

Resigned, I sat back in my chair. When dealing with George, it was sometimes easier just to let him rant. He'd run out of steam eventually.

"Didn't that property have a VW bug ram its front porches last year?"

"Yes. And the prior insurance company paid for all new porches. That's a good thing for us."

"And wasn't there serious water damage the year before which was caused by a negligent tenant? Ruined his floors and the ceiling below him. That must have cost big bucks. Then there was the damage from an illegal fire pit in the back yard. And now this fire."

"The negligent tenant no longer lives there. And again, prior damage was covered by the prior insurance company. And repaired. The only alleged issue now is the occupancy. And that will change as soon as the new owner does some work, most of which is cosmetic. Tell me, what's your point?"

"My point is you made a big mistake pushing Underwriting to accept such a risk. It showed very poor judgment on your part. The policy is only a few months old. And this fire could cost us a bundle. You'll be lucky to keep your job after this. That's my point."

And he appeared to be relishing the situation.

My assistant Peggy burst into my office, slightly out of breath. "Hi Amy. Glad I caught you. There are a few things I need to discuss with you right away." She held up a few manila files folders. "Would you excuse us, George?"

He growled. "You'll have to take a number. Amy and I are not quite finished here."

"Not to worry. I don't mind waiting." Peggy plopped into a chair, a big grin on her face.

George glared at her, but continued his mini-inquisition. "Tell me about the fire damage, Amy. Do you have a figure yet?"

"The appraiser and I are meeting at the property later this morning." I already had a good idea on the subject, but I was damned if I'd volunteer any information. Better simply to answer George's questions and let him discover the rest for himself. If he could.

"Who's assigned to the case?" he asked.

"Nick Quigley."

George rolled his eyes. "Isn't he the appraiser who's in your back pocket? The guy who says and does whatever you want him to?"

I chose not to respond to such drivel.

He continued. "And then there's the other side of the problem."

My ears perked up, curious to know where he might be going with this. "And what would that be?"

"The amount of time you've been spending out of the office. What about the rest of your job? There's no way you could keep up with issues in here when you're hardly ever around." He crossed his arms across his chest.

I chose to respond to this charge. "I speak with Peggy several times a day. She keeps me up-to-date on life here. She's also doing a fabulous job training Tiffany. I'm so glad I asked her to help you out with that. You didn't appear to have enough time to devote to it." *Or the will to do so.*

He balled his hands into tight little fists.

I continued. "As for things which come up, I believe you are capable of dealing with many of them. If not, you can always call my cell. And don't worry. I am spending time in the evenings working on the up-coming job reviews. I wouldn't want to be late with your evaluation." I was lying about this, but did have plans to deal with his job review shortly.

My turn to cross my arms.

"Right." he stood and slithered toward the door.

I followed him and closed the door behind him. "Thanks, Peg. You're a lifesaver." I sank into my chair.

"My pleasure. I'm only sorry I didn't get here sooner. I was showing Tiffany how to work the new email system. I'm guessing George gave you an earful. He's been looking forward to doing so since he learned about the fire."

"Don't worry. I can handle George."

"Much to his chagrin." Peggy grinned.

"That's for sure. What do you have for me?" I pointed to the folders in her hands.

"Nothing. These were just for show. To make sure George would leave."

I laughed. "What would I ever do without you?"

"Let's hope you never get to find out. I need this job. And like it. Now, please, fill me in on what's been happening. Don't leave anything out."

I looked at my watch. "We'll have to make it quick. Mark said he wanted to speak with me first thing in the morning. And he meant yesterday morning."

"Not to worry on that score. Mark called a few minutes ago. Said he's running late. He should be in around nine thirty. We've got plenty of time."

Peggy and I spent the next half hour discussing the events of the past two days. I gave her all the gory details from Chadwick Street as well as the good news that Sam was doing just fine. She caught me up on all the latest office gossip, much of it about me and/or George. We had a few chuckles, many of them at George's expense. Then it was time for me to make my way to Executive Heaven and let Mark know what was really happening.

CHAPTER 16

took the stairs, all five flights of them, using the time to get my thoughts organized. The exercise couldn't hurt either. Mark's door was open when I arrived.

He greeted me without a smile. "Come in, Amy. Have a seat. It's good to see you."

He didn't say "finally" but I heard the word just the same. Mark and I had a weird sort of relationship with him being both my boss and my best friend Nancy's husband. Somehow he managed to handle both roles separately, almost as if he were two distinct people. That was a skill I hadn't yet mastered. Today Mark-my-boss was making me uncomfortable.

"Correct me if I'm wrong," he said, "but weren't we supposed to meet yesterday morning?"

I steeled myself and said, "Right. I'm really sorry. But when I tell you why I didn't make it into the office, I'm sure you'll understand."

He cleared his throat. "OK. Let's start at the beginning. Monday morning. You learned there was a fire at a property we recently insured. Against our better judgment. As a favor to a friend of yours. How am I doing so far?"

The tone of his voice said a lot more than his words. "You're doing fine."

I sat very straight and waited for the rest of his grilling. There was no way I'd let him know how intimidating he could be.

"And you dashed out of here to see the fire for yourself. Unusual behavior for you, Amy. I mean, you do dash out of here fairly often, and for an interesting variety of reasons, but you seldom seem to feel the need to visit the scene of a fire, particularly when it has barely been extinguished. No, such behavior is not like you at all. Tell me, please, what was so different about this particular fire?"

So far I was seeing more curiosity than anger from him. A good sign. "For starters, it involved a friend of mine. I thought that merited a little extra attention."

"O.K. I can understand that." He consulted some notes on his desk. "George appeared to think the building might be a total loss."

"George was mistaken. He didn't have all the facts, or any of them actually. He sometimes tends to overreact and jump to conclusions." I had to watch what I said here. Mark tended to frown on employees bad-mouthing each other, even if one of them was a total jerk and the other was nearly always in the right.

"The fire began in the cellar," I continued, "which has a dirt floor and is only used for storage. There's not a lot to damage down there. A couple of windows blew out, but that's pretty much it. The firefighters arrived quickly. They got the blaze under control before it had a chance to spread very far. One of the first floor apartments was involved. There's damage to the walls and the floors. The front door and some first floor windows need to be replaced. And that's it. Otherwise, it's mostly smoke issues throughout the rest of the building. I'll be getting ServPro out there as quickly as possible."

Mark sat down and exhaled noisily. "That is good news."

"Right. I don't have a dollar figure for you yet. One of the appraisers is meeting me there later today. I'll know more after speaking with him."

Mark paid attention. He calmed down. He took notes. He was, after all, a reasonable guy. "From what you're saying, we're probably not in bad shape."

"Agreed. I made sure Andy had enough coverage when I helped him write the policy. He wanted a large deductible to keep the cost down. I talked him out of it. I'm glad I did. Otherwise, the poor guy would be in a mess now."

Mark frowned. "NEC&I would have been in better shape if he'd taken a larger deductible."

Mark was right, of course, but so was I. "That's true. But I couldn't advise a friend to do something which wasn't in his best interest."

"I get that. I don't like it, but I do get it. The friend in me understands perfectly. The boss in me isn't all that thrilled. And none of this explains why you've been among the missing for two entire days."

I gave him my 'I'm in control of this' look. It felt good. "This is where the story gets interesting."

He raised his eyebrows. "How so?"

"There was a body found in the cellar. A Canadian college student who was down here for a fencing tournament. Which means now this has become more of a police matter."

"What!" He jumped to his feet and glared at me. "How awful! Nobody told me anything about a body." He paced around his office, a serious look on his face. "A fencer? As in someone who duels with swords?"

"Exactly," I responded.

"Who was he? What was he doing in the cellar? Was he one of Mr. Yesley's tenants? How did he die?"

"The fellow didn't die due to the fire. He was stabbed. It appears to be murder." I went on to explain the events of the past few days in excruciating detail.

Mark hung his head. "Good Lord, Amy. What a mess. And from a business point of view, it makes me wonder if we might be on the hook for a wrongful death suit here."

"From what I've learned so far, I would say no."

Mark's whole body relaxed visibly. "That's a relief."

"Agreed. There is something else though."

His eyes widened. "Do I want to hear this?"

"Probably not, but here goes." I told him about the baby's body.

He listened, eyes wide. "Horrible. Simply horrible. Now I understand why you haven't been around. It's almost as if that house is cursed."

"Well, let's hope the curse has run its course."

"Amen to that." He frowned. "What got George so fired up?"

I shook my head. "I hate to say this, and you probably don't want to hear it, but George never got over the fact I was promoted over him. Now he delights in anything he thinks might make me look bad. I usually manage to ignore it and find a way to work with the guy. Sometimes it isn't easy."

"Thanks for telling me that. I had no idea there was bad blood between the two of you. I always knew George had a sour disposition but looked beyond it because the man is good at what he does. He makes a positive contribution to the company."

And a negative contribution to employee morale. I decided to keep this thought to myself.

Mark paused and made a few notes. "I understand how you must feel. But you need to see my position here. I have to weigh the value of the job the man does against the effect he has on the staff. It can be a tough call. And until I make that call, we'll all have to handle things as best we can."

"You mean suck it up and make nice?" *Definitely not my first choice.*

"Unfortunately, yes." He made another note. "And please let me know what dollar figure the appraiser comes up with. Also continue to keep me in the loop on the police activity. Just in case it might involve NEC&I."

"Will do. And, by the way, please keep the news about the baby to yourself for now. The police don't want to release that information just yet."

"Understood."

I smiled. The third degree was over. And I was still in Mark's good graces. "So tell me, how is Nancy doing? I haven't spoken with her in nearly a week. Is she feeling any better?"

He shook his head. "The darn morning sickness is still giving her a hard time. She never complains, though. She's so happy to be having this baby. And her first trimester is almost over. They say it gets better from there."

"Please give her my love. And tell her I'll call soon."

"And stay away from George for a while, Amy. We need to keep the peace around here. You don't want to say or do anything foolish."

Don't be so sure about that. If the man crosses me again, perhaps I won't be able to restrain myself.

CHAPTER 17

I left the office and headed over to Chadwick Street to meet with Nick Quigley. He was a good guy as well as an experienced appraiser. I was confident he'd give Andy a fair settlement without any undue pressure from me. And I hoped he'd do so quickly. Andy needed the money.

Nick was waiting for me on the sidewalk. I waved to Mrs. Czwakiel and her friend Beatrice on the porch next door, then joined Nick. "How are you?" I said. "I hope I didn't keep you waiting."

"Not at all," he replied. "Just got here myself."

"Thanks for fitting me into your schedule. I've got a personal interest in this loss, so I really appreciate your help." I might as well be up-front with Nick from the get-go. To hell with what George may think.

"Not a problem," he said. "My caseload is a little light at the moment. The snowbirds have gone south for the winter. The folks who are still here are hibernating."

"As you can see, the front door is out of commission. We need to get into the property from around back," I told him. "The cellar is still off-limits, but there's not much to see there anyway. We can deal with that another time."

I gave Nick a quick tour of the building and what damage I was aware of, then left him alone to do his job. I trusted the guy. He was good at what he did.

I headed back outside in the hope that Mrs. Czwakiel might once again have some interesting tidbit to share with me. The woman certainly didn't miss much.

She hailed me from her front porch. "Hello, Amy. Do you have a few minutes to chat?"

"I've always got time for you," I said. "How are you today?"

"As good as a body can be at my age, right Beatrice?"

Beatrice nodded.

Mrs. Czwakiel leaned toward me, "There's something I need to tell you," she said in a conspiratorial whisper.

"Oh?" *Please tell me it's something that will help my case.*

"It happened again. I was up in the night. Trouble sleeping again. What can you do? Old age is no walk in the park. I went into the kitchen to make myself a nice cup of chamomile tea. That's when I saw a light behind Andy's house. Somebody was trying to get in again. What do you think about that?"

I thought that it was not a good development. Or was it simply the woman's imagination on overdrive? "Was there enough light for you to identify the intruder?"

She shook her head. "No. It was too dark. But I'm guessing it was that nasty Florescu fellow. He's been hanging around the neighborhood at all hours trying to get into the house ever since the fire. What do you suppose he wants in there?"

"Let's hope we find out soon. Did you call the police?"

"Of course," she said. "And just like the last time, he was gone by the time they got here. The police are going to think I'm nothing but a crazy old lady who doesn't have enough to do."

"Even though that's exactly what you are," Beatrice chimed in with a chuckle. "It's a tough job, but somebody has to do it."

Mrs. Czwakiel scowled at her friend.

I stayed out of that conversation.

"Good afternoon, Ladies," a voice from the sidewalk said. I turned to see Douglas Weiss walking toward the front steps of Andy's house. Maybe still looking for his mail.

Beatrice squinted and stared at him. "Hello, Dick. How are you? It's been a very long time. What brings you here?"

A cloud passed over Weiss's face. "I'm afraid you're mistaking me for somebody else, Ma'am. My name is Douglas Weiss." He hurried away.

Beatrice watched him leave, shaking her head. "I could have sworn that was Dick. You know who I mean, don't you, Helen? He used to live in number twelve. Had a nice wife. Pretty girl. Remember?"

Mrs. Czwakiel smiled at her. "Sorry. No I don't. Maybe you're just confused." She pulled her glasses out of a pocket and looked across the street. "Oh, look. Here come the boys." She pointed to James and Ryan making their way in our direction.

"Do I know them?" Beatrice asked.

"Of course you do, Bea. The gay couple from across the street. The nice fellows with the big dog named Fifi."

"Oh, yes. Of course. Hello boys."

"Good afternoon to you, Ladies," Ryan said.

"How are you today?" Mrs. Czwakiel asked.

"Not so good," James responded, his words catching in his throat.

A good look at the two of them confirmed that something was amiss. Gone were the stylish outfits they'd been sporting the other day. And the impeccable grooming. Their clothing looked like they'd slept in it, though their pale, drawn faces suggested that they may not have slept at all.

"James and I have had a difficult morning, truly tragic," Ryan told us.

"And extremely upsetting," James added. His eyes glistened with tears.

"Oh dear," Mrs. Czwakiel said. "What's the matter?"

"Something horrible has happened." Ryan's voice shook as he spoke. "It's Fifi." He sobbed. "She's in bad shape."

"What happened?" Mrs. Czwakiel asked. "Did she get hit by a car or something?"

"She was beaten," James sobbed. "Badly beaten. We found her in her play yard when we got home last night. She was bleeding and in obvious pain. Our poor little girl. It was dreadful to see her suffering like that. She's in Angel Memorial Hospital now."

"I'm so sorry," I said. "Is she going to be all right?"

Ryan sobbed. "The vet told us she may pull through, but it's too soon to tell. He just can't be sure yet. We simply don't know what we'd ever do without her."

James reached out and squeezed Ryan's shoulder. "Hang in there, my friend. Fifi's as tough as she is sweet. I just know she'll make it."

"Have you reported this to the police?" I asked.

"Of course," James said. "That's where we're coming from just now."

"Do you have any idea who may have done this?" I asked.

Ryan's eyes clouded over. "There's only one person we know of who didn't care for Fifi. That dreadful Florescu fellow. It had to be him."

It seemed as if everybody was blaming Florescu for everything. I needed to learn how much of it was true. And fast.

CHAPTER 18

I left James, Ryan and the neighbor ladies when Detective Donnelly arrived along with a uniformed officer I didn't recognize.

"Hello, Detective. And how are you this lovely day?"

He frowned at me. "Good morning, Ms. Lynch. Let's get this show on the road. I have a busy day ahead of me."

"I'd be happy to fill in for you if there's someplace else you need to be," I offered.

"No way." He scowled at me. "I need to be here for a number of reasons. Serious reasons. I also want to see the fencing team one more time. To wish them a safe trip home."

I couldn't resist asking, "You mean to make one last check for a guilty look on somebody's face? Do you actually suspect any of them?"

"Not really," he said. "But I've been fooled before. Once. I'm not going to let it happen again. And I do have one piece of good news for you."

That was a relief. "What?"

"The fencer who had gone missing, Robert Poirier, has been found. A state trooper picked him up hitchhiking on Route 93 Monday night. Seems the guy was trying to make his way back to Montréal. He wouldn't talk to anybody at first. They had him in custody over twenty-four hours before he explained what he was up to and why."

"And that was …?"

"He said he panicked when he learned that the Boston Police were coming to the fencing club to question them. He had drugs on him. Hard drugs. Cocaine. Fentanyl. Said he had sold cocaine to Howie Zupkoff on New Year's Eve. Zupkoff wanted more at the tournament the next day. Poirier refused. They argued. Zupkoff threated to rat on him. No wonder he panicked and took off the next day when he heard that Zupkoff was dead and the police were coming. It turns out Poirier also had a juvenile record for assault. Once the kid came clean, the state cops contacted his parents in Canada. They came right down to bring him home."

"At least we know he's safe," I said. "And there's one less thing for us to worry about."

"True," Donnelly said. "But I bet he's off the fencing team. No way any coach would put up with a bad actor like that."

"If he were my kid, I'd lock him in his room until his twenty-first birthday."

Donnelly actually smiled at that.

Freddy and his fencing team pulled up in two vans. They were a somber-looking group. Only four days ago, Freddy had arrived with his team of eight fencers. Today he was heading back to Montréal with only six of them. Howie Zupkoff's body would be shipped home for burial once the post mortem was completed, even though the cause of death was obvious. And as Donnelly had just told me, the police were dealing with Robert Poirier. The remaining team members looked a bit worse for the wear. No small wonder after days of camping out at the fencing club.

Freddy herded them out of the vans and onto the sidewalk. "Wait here and do whatever the police tell you," he said to them. He gave me a quick hug. "Hello, Amy. Thanks for being here. It's good for the kids to see a friendly face."

Detective Donnelly addressed me and Freddy. "Here's the plan. Officer Santos and I will escort the fencers into the building one at a time. Or actually two, one with him and one with me. You two will supervise the others as they wait here until it's their turn."

I agreed, though I was pretty sure the team didn't need much supervision.

"Someone will need to take care of Robert Poirier's things, and Howie Zupkoff's," I reminded him.

Detective Donnelly said, "I'll see that they do." He turned to the fencers and explained the plan to them, then he and Officer Santos escorted the first two fencers inside.

"How are these guys doing?" I asked Freddy.

"Hanging in there," he told me. "This trip has been an ordeal for them, but they're tougher than they look. The young often are."

I faced the fencers, feeling somewhat like the high school teacher I had been fifteen years ago. These kids weren't much older than my students. I even used my schoolteacher voice. It had always been helpful in maintaining order. And it could be heard for several blocks. "Hi, guys. Remember me? I met you at the pizza party the other night."

"Some party," a voice from the rear said. "Next time, let's not invite the cops."

Everybody groaned.

"I'm sure you're all eager to get home," I said. "These past few days have been tough on you."

Nobody argued with that.

"Definitely not your run-of-the-mill tournament trip," somebody in the rear said.

The mousy girl with glasses added, "Right. We usually leave with the same number of people we had when we arrived." She choked back a sob.

The chubby fellow said, "I never thought I'd be happy to be heading back to school."

"Things weren't all bad," the petite blonde girl said. "We had a good time touring Boston the other day."

"The Museum of Science was pretty cool," the freckled face red-head added. "And Andy and his friend Pete sang to us on the Duck Boat tour."

Freddy groaned. "I was hoping you'd forget that."

The team fell into a glum silence.

I struggled to think of something to distract the fencers. Anything which could lighten the mood a bit. The best I could come up with was "You know, I've been thinking about taking some fencing lessons myself. I wonder if you guys could give me a few pointers. And perhaps explain a few things to me."

At least that got their attention.

"Like what?" the red-headed fellow asked.

I wracked my brains for a moment, then said, "Like why do people hold their rear arm up when they're fencing?"

That produced a lot of blank looks from the kids. Freddy jumped in to fill the silence. "It's tradition, going back to the days when dueling was illegal and usually took place in the dark. The back arm was used to hold a lantern."

Interesting. I believed duels were still illegal, but kept that thought to myself. I turned to the kids again. "What is the first thing I need to learn?"

"En garde!" the four of them replied in unison as they all assumed the initial fencing stance.

I did so as well. "Like this?"

"Right," the heavy fellow said, "then you have to learn to advance, parry, retreat and lunge."

My improvised lesson was cut short by the return of the police and the two fenders toting their bags. The two girls followed the police in next. The glum silence returned.

Andy gave me a weak smile. "That was a good try, Amy. At least it helped for a while."

We were all milling around restlessly when a ruckus broke out in the back hard. Everybody rushed to see what was happening.

Detective Donnelly and the other officer were wrestling with someone I didn't recognize—a rather scruffy looking fellow with greasy black hair and an ugly tattoo on his neck, wearing torn jeans and a dungaree jacket. Definitely not one of Freddy's fencers.

The team stood off to the side, watching in horrified silence.

"Fucking cops," the fellow shouted. "Get your filthy hands off me."

"Watch your mouth," Donnelly responded. "And step away from the house."

"Make me," the fellow taunted as he continued toward the rear door.

Donnelly grabbed his arm. "You can't go in there."

"Oh yes I can," the fellow snarled at him. "Just watch me." He pulled away from Donnelly. "I got every right to. There's stuff of mine in there. I need to get it."

Donnelly said, "Settle down, Buddy. We'll get it for you. We're limiting access to the building at the moment. Do you live here?"

My turn to speak up. "No he doesn't."

"Don't listen to that bitch," the fellow said to Donnelly. "What the Hell does she know? I live here with my girlfriend. And she asked me to come by to pick up some of her things."

Aha! This fellow had to be the ever-popular Charlie Florescu, Ellen James's unpleasant boyfriend. And he was every bit as charming as people had described. Probably also as high as a proverbial kite. Why else would he defy the police like that? He pulled himself free from Officer Santos and dashed toward the house.

Donnelly lunged at him. A couple of fencers stepped forward to help. Donnelly motioned them away. "Step back, guys. We don't want anybody getting hurt here. I can handle this guy," he said. In no time at all, Donnelly pinned the would-be intruder's arms behind his back while the other cop handcuffed him. They made a good team.

"Let me go!" the fellow shouted. "I've got rights here. And I need to get into that house."

"What's going on here?" A voice called from the sidewalk.

I turned to see Andy on his way up the street. "Is there a problem?" he asked.

Donnelly responded. "This fellow wanted to gain access to the building. He didn't like it when I said he couldn't do that."

"I'm glad you folks were here to stop him," Andy said. "He doesn't live here. I've never seen him before."

What's your name, Bud?" Donnelly asked.

"Florescu," the boy growled. "Charlie Florescu."

It was interesting to see Florescu in person. I hoped I'd get a chance to ask him a few questions – about the fire, the late Howie Zupkoff, the attack on Fifi. So many things he might help clear up for me. But that would have to wait.

"He has no right to be here," Andy told Donnelly, "And from what I've heard, this guy is bad news. But I would like to speak with him for a minute."

Donnelly rolled his eyes. "Go ahead."

"What the fuck do you want with me?" Florescu glared at Andy.

"I want to know where Ellen is," Andy said. "I've been trying to locate her. Can you tell me where I can find her?"

"I ain't telling you nothing," Florescu spat. "It's none of your damn business."

"OK. That's enough," Donnelly said to Florescu. He led his prisoner to the car. "Maybe you'll be more cooperative at the station. Now wait in the car with Officer Santos while we finish up our business here." He turned to Andy on the sidewalk. "How about we go see if we can find whatever Mr. Florescu was looking for? Which apartment is it?"

"I'll show you. It's this way." Andy and Donnelly headed around to the back door.

I sat on the front steps to catch my breath, wondering what they'd find in the apartment and hoping it was enough to keep Florescu in jail for a long time.

Andy and Donnelly were back in a flash, their arms loaded with packages of what appeared to be white butcher paper. My guess was that they didn't contain meat.

"Drugs," Donnelly announced. "The freezer was full of them. Big stash of cash as well. I can't believe my folks missed these when they checked the building the other day. Gotta have a talk with those guys. And, by the way, that apartment is now a crime scene until further notice. Everybody stay clear of it."

I couldn't believe the detective had announced all this in front of Freddy and his team. Not ideal police procedure. And he was ordering me around as well. Go figure.

Donnelly turned to Andy and scowled. "We missed you at the station yesterday afternoon, Mr. Yesley. We were expecting you at 5:00. What happened? Did you change your mind about speaking with us?"

Andy actually slapped his forehead with the heel of his hand. "Holy crap, Detective! I forgot all about it. Sorry."

"Sorry won't cut it. Please follow us there now. We need to have a serious chat. Unless you'd rather ride with us in the squad car."

"That's OK, Detective. I'll follow you."

I watched with mixed emotions as Donnelly loaded the evidence into the trunk of the squad car and sped off with Andy right behind. I liked Andy. I trusted him. Why didn't the police? What did they know that I didn't? And how was I going to break the news to Pete that his cousin might be in trouble?

CHAPTER 19

I said my good-byes to Freddy and his fencers and made my way to the office. I had barely begun reading my mountain of mail when Peggy and Tiffany marched in, Tiffany with a triumphant look on her face. That was nice to see. Not very long ago, the girl showed up in my office in tears at least once a week. She'd come a long way since then. She had shown a lot of initiative and gone above and beyond her job description on several occasions. I was actually beginning to rely on her. I credited Peggy for Tiffany's growing confidence. Peggy was a gem.

"You two ladies look quite pleased with yourselves. What's up?"

They both grinned and held up some papers.

"Have a seat," I told them. "Whatever it is you have there, I sure hope it's good news."

They sat.

Peggy spoke first. "Tiffany did a stellar job researching Andrew Yesley's tenants. And she had some interesting thoughts about what she learned. I wanted her to present the information to you herself."

Peggy was always generous with her praise, quick to give credit where credit was due.

"Sounds good to me." I smiled at Tiffany. "Tell me what you found."

Tiffany beamed at me and referred to her notes. "I ran all three tenants' credit reports, as well as their history with the Registry of Motor Vehicles. I also did google searches on each of them and searched for them on Facebook. Ursula Fagan has spotty credit, though no bankruptcies or major debt issues. Just the normal stuff. There was nothing on her in the Registry database. I also checked as many out-of-state DMVs as I could access. Still nothing. Ergo, it's likely the woman didn't drive."

Ergo? Had Tiffany been studying Latin in her spare time? Or perhaps law? "What about Ellen James and Douglas Weiss?"

Peggy laughed. "That's when things start to get interesting."

"How so?"

"Ellen James has at least six credit cards and fabulous credit," Tiffany said. "Absolutely nothing negative anywhere. She also has an extensive RMV history. A multitude of minor incidents and infractions over the past few years."

That sounded good so far. "And …?" I prodded, waiting for the other shoe to drop.

"In the last twelve months, the girl was cited six times for possession of a Class D substance with intent to distribute."

I stopped her here. "But wait right there. One of the neighbors said that she didn't have a car. None of the tenants did."

"That's true," Tiffany agreed. "Both Ellen's license and her registration were cancelled two years ago. Her vehicle is now registered to somebody named Florescu."

No big shock there, but good to know.

"I can't exactly prove this," Tiffany continued, "but I suspect Ellen may be in a cash business, possibly selling drugs if the RMV info is accurate. Her Facebook page gives her occupation as 'Lady of Leisure.'"

That was a bit of a leap, but anything was possible. I decided not to rain on Tiffany's parade until I knew more. I'd ask Andy how Ellen paid her rent – by check or cash.

Tiffany continued. "I also checked voter registration records. No Ellen James there. "I guess some people just aren't civic minded."

"What about the other tenants?" I asked.

"Ursula Fagan is a model citizen. She has been a regular voter for years."

"What about Douglas Weiss?"

Tiffany shook her head. "I found absolutely nothing on him. No credit report, no driver's license. Nothing. Anywhere."

"It's like the man's a ghost," Peggy said. "No records of him that we can find on any database I can access. It's not normal. It's as if he dropped out of the sky a couple of months ago."

"And landed on Chadwick Street," I said, becoming all the more curious about the man.

"I'm wondering if he's in the witness protection program," Tiffany said.

"Interesting thought, Tiffany." *Either that or he just moved here from out-of-state and didn't get a driver's license yet. Or register to vote.* But I held my tongue. No sense deflating Tiffany's bubble. Just in case she was right.

CHAPTER 20

Andy showed up at my door just as Peggy and Tiffany were leaving. He looked even worse than he had earlier, exhausted and sad and worried all at the same time.

"Andy, hi. Come on in."

He seemed a bit unsteady on his feet.

"Have a seat," I told him. "What's going on?"

He collapsed into my visitor's chair and put his head in his hands.

I gave him a minute to compose himself, then said, "Is it really that bad?"

"Even worse than you think." He shook his head. "Worse than I ever imagined it could be. It's all totally unreal. I don't know what to think anymore. Pete's in court today so now I'm dumping my troubles on you. Sorry."

"There's nothing to apologize for. You know I'm here to help. Did the police give you a tough time?"

"Like you wouldn't believe. It was horrible. I wish to Hell I'd asked Pete to go with me. I thought they just wanted information from me. Boy was I ever mistaken. They treated me like a suspect."

"Why didn't you refuse to answer questions their questions without a lawyer present?"

"Because I knew Pete was tied up today. And I thought it would make me look more guilty than they already thought I was if I tried to put off speaking with them."

Bad choice, for sure, but it was too late to worry about that. Andy was kind and generous, but perhaps not over-bright. "Tell me about it," I said.

"I asked them outright if they suspected me of something. They said it seemed I might possibly be involved somehow, either me or one of my tenants. Or perhaps one of the fencers."

"Why?"

"They said it had to be someone with access to the inside of the house."

"Did you tell them about the broken lock on the front door?"

"Oh yeah. But I think that just made matters worse."

That came as no surprise.

"Then they put me through the third degree. And their questions were all over the place. What kind of security measures had I taken at the property? How well did I know my tenants? How long had the tenants lived there? Did they pay their rent in cash or by check? Where are they now so they can be questioned?"

Things I'd like to know as well.

Andy continued, "They asked how long had I owned the building? How well did I know the prior owner?"

"These are actually good questions Andy. What did you tell them?"

"I gave them the prior owner's name. He's deceased. I bought the house from his estate."

Bummer. That meant we couldn't ask the guy about the ammo in the cellar.

"Then they got into my finances," Andy continued. "Things like how much did I pay for the property? How much did I borrow?

What are my monthly mortgage payments? How much are the taxes? How expensive would the renovations be? How was I planning to pay for them? How was I going to get by with no income until the renovations are done? How much rent had I been collecting? Was I planning to increase rents any time soon?"

"They certainly were thorough." *Maybe more so than necessary. Or maybe not. Did the police know something I didn't?*

"But why?" Andy asked. "What do they care about my finances? That should be none of their business. Do they think I started the fire to collect the insurance money?" His voice rose as he spoke until he was nearly shouting.

"If you were in financial trouble, that could be viewed as a possible motive. But I'm sure they don't really think that, Andy. They're just doing their jobs, documenting the files to cover their backsides." I hoped I sounded more confident about this than I felt. What Andy needed at the moment was reassurance. And a long talk with his cousin Pete about dealing with authorities.

He sucked in a big breath then let it out slowly. "You sure?"

"Pretty sure, yeah. We do that here all the time."

"They want to know if I have any enemies. Can you believe that?"

Actually I could, but I chose not to say so.

"They even asked me if I smoked marijuana. As if I'd admit it if I did. What do you think about that?"

I shrugged. "I guess they're just covering all bases. Though I don't know why they'd care about that. It is legal in Massachusetts."

He frowned. "Then they started in on Freddy and his team staying there. How well did I know Freddy? Did I trust him? Did I charge them money to camp out on the second floor? Had I ever met the kids on the fencing team before? Could Freddy vouch for all of them? What did I know about the fellow who went missing? Was I acquainted with the deceased fencer? What did I know about him?

Good grief. Are they trying to blame me for his death as well? Do they think I stabbed the guy?"

"They can't possibly think that. You have an air-tight alibi. You were at the tournament all day. I'm sure dozens of people saw you there. We've got no worries on that score." At least I could assure him of something.

"I guess you're right." He was silent for a moment. "I can't deal with any of this right now. Let's talk about something else. How is the claim going? What happens next?"

"I'm trying hard to get it moving. I want to get you some money as soon as possible." And I was pretty sure I could make that happen, one way or another.

"That'd be great, Amy. Money was tight to begin with. The way things are going now, it can only get worse."

"I expect to hear back from the appraiser shortly with his estimate for the clean-up and repairs. He's a good guy. I know him well. I'll ask him to do what he can to hurry things along." I listened to what I'd just said and cringed. Was George right? Did I have Nick Quigley in my back pocket? I hate it when George might be right.

Andy interrupted my thoughts. "That'd be a big help. And I have some news on my tenants. That's the only positive development at the moment."

We certainly needed something positive right about now. "Were you able to contact them?"

"I had a conversation with Doug Weiss. He's staying at a motel on Gallivan Boulevard, but can't afford it for much longer. The poor guy is only working part-time right now. At the Dunkin' down the street. He doesn't have a car. Needs to walk to work or get a job on a bus line. I gave him a small loan to tide him over."

Which you probably couldn't afford. "You're a nice person, Andy."

"I try," he said. "I spoke with Ursula Fagan again. She plans to stay at her daughter's. She has already moved most of her clothes and personal items there. Her daughter is coming by some time next week or two to look at what's left. She won't be taking the furniture. I guess I'll try to donate it somewhere. Wouldn't want to let anything usable go to waste."

"Good idea." *If it didn't reek of smoke.*

"What about the third tenant? Ellen, right?" I asked.

"I keep trying her phone. I've left several messages. So far, no return call," he told me.

"Let's hope she turns up sometime soon. Maybe you could speak with that creepy boyfriend of hers. What's-his-name, Florescu? At least we know where he is at the moment, safely in police custody."

"That is a relief."

"What about ServPro?" I asked. "Did you hear from them yet? Were you able to schedule them?"

"They're starting tomorrow morning. On the second floor. I plan to work right along with them as much as I can. Maybe that'll save me a little money. It will also speed things up. As a matter of fact, I'm planning on doing as much of the clean-up work as I can, repainting and so forth, myself. No sense paying people to do things I can handle myself."

"I have some good news for you on that score."

He looked up, his eyes a bit more hopeful.

"NEC&I will pay you for any work you do yourself, and at the going rate."

His shoulders relaxed. "Wow. That is good news. Thanks, Amy."

"It's standard procedure. Oh, and by the way, be sure to keep the ServPro team out of Ellen's apartment. Don't forget, that's a crime scene until we hear differently."

"Gotcha."

"It's going to be all right, Andy," I told him. "We're all professionals here. Me, the appraiser, the police, not to mention the folks at ServPro. We've got your back. I promise."

He flashed me a small smile. "Thanks Amy. I sure hope you're right."

I hoped so too.

The way the police had questioned Andy had me second-guessing my thoughts about him. I didn't like the way that made me feel. And I didn't want to mention it to Pete. At least not yet.

CHAPTER 21

As late as it was in the afternoon, there was still paperwork I needed to handle before George found another reason to tattle on me to Mark. I was making good progress when my phone rang. It was Nancy.

"Hi Stranger," I said. "Believe it or not, I was going to call you later."

"I beat you to it. It's been too long since we had a good old-fashioned heart-to-heart. As much as I like staying at home, I do miss seeing you every day."

I knew the feeling. We were the best of friends. Nancy had always been a wonderful sounding board for me. "How are you doing?" She'd had a difficult time conceiving and had already suffered one miscarriage. I prayed she'd do better this time. She and Mark wanted a baby badly. And I was more than ready to be an honorary aunt.

"I'm better every day."

"That's good to hear. When you're up to it, let's plan lunch, or a shopping extravaganza or dinner. Or maybe all three. We haven't had fun together in ages."

"Sounds like a plan." She paused. "I tried to call you at home. Tell me, why are you still at the office? It's nearly 6:00."

Good question, for which I had a good answer. "Things have been busy here lately. I've been out in the field a lot, and I need to keep up with my paperwork and other such boring functions. You know how it is."

Nancy laughed. "After ten years of working with you, I do indeed know. Mark told me what's been going on with you and George. Sounds like things are heating up between you folks. Fill me in. You know I love a good fight."

"That's the main reason I'm still here," I said. "I don't want to give George any ammunition. His job review is due this week. I'm trying to get it over with before he starts bitching about his raise being late. The trouble is, I'm struggling with how to approach his performance. It isn't easy to be fair and impartial with the guy when most of the time I want to wring his scrawny neck. Do you have any brilliant ideas?"

There was a moment of quiet. Then Nancy said, "Actually, I do. I learned a few tricks while working in Human Resources this past year. You could take a different approach."

"Out with it. I'm all ears." I'd take any help I could get.

"It's simple. Give the guy what he wants."

No way in Hell. "Please tell me you're kidding. What George wants most is my job."

"Maybe not," Nancy said. "Maybe he just wants a little recognition. Everybody needs to feel appreciated. And he does handle some parts of his job rather well."

"True, but ..."

"But nothing, Amy. Listen to me. This can work. Acknowledge what he does well. He'll eat it up."

"OK. I get that. But what about the rest? He truly sucks at some parts of his job."

"Then give him enough rope to hang himself."

My ears perked up at the thought of a lynching. Then my conscience kicked in. "Run that by me again?"

"Make it sound like you're giving the guy a well-deserved promotion. Give him some additional duties. Stuff he's good at and enjoys. Let him feel like the company needs him, that he's the only one who can do whatever it is you come up with. He'll either rise to the occasion or he won't. But it'll be his doing."

"I like the way you think. This could actually work." And I could come out smelling like a rose.

"But wait," Nancy said. "There's more. Also tell him that in return he needs to attend some sort of sensitivity or customer service seminar."

"You're kidding! One of those happy horseshit classes? He'd hate that." *And I'd love to see him hating it.*

"He will. But he'll do it if he wants the rest of the deal. And don't forget, happy horseshit is the stuff of which excellent customer service is made. Just let him think you need him. That's all he really wants."

I gave this some thought. "Actually, I do need him for certain things. But that doesn't mean I like him. Or ever will."

"And that's OK."

"You're a genius Nancy. This could be fun."

"Let me know how it goes."

"Thanks. Will do. I'll talk to you soon." I hung up the phone and dashed off to meet Pete and Andy for a quick dinner before heading home to work on George's review.

When I arrived at the Ashmont Grill in Dorchester, Pete and Andy were not only already seated, but also well into their first beer, or perhaps their second for all I knew. "Good evening, guys. How're you doing?"

Pete stood and gave me a quick kiss. Andy saluted me with his beer.

The waiter came by with a menu for me. I ordered a glass of Sauvignon Blanc. "What's happening?" I asked.

Pete looked at Andy.

Andy put down his glass. "Doug Weiss called me a little while ago with a proposal. Like I told you, he's only working part-time right now, not making much money. He can't afford to stay at the motel any longer. Or pay first and last months' rent on a new place. He wants to move back into Chadwick Street."

"Isn't the building still a crime scene? At least parts of it?" I asked.

"That's right," Andy said. "I know I can't let him move back in right now, but the guy's got nowhere to go and no money to get there. I'd like to find a way to help him."

The waiter came by to deliver my wine and take our orders. Rigatoni Bolognese for Andy. Pan seared salmon for Pete.

"That salmon sounds good," I said. "I'll have the same." I raised my glass. "Here's to better days for all of us."

"I'll drink to that," Andy said. He drained his beer glass, signaled to the waiter for another and turned to me. "I need your advice on something, Amy."

"Sure. What's up?"

"It's about Weiss." Andy stopped speaking and stared at his hands.

I waited to hear more.

Pete spoke up. "Andy and I are having a slight difference of opinion on something."

"What?" I asked.

"Helping Weiss."

Andy dropped his fork and raised his voice. "The guy needs a break, Pete."

"I get that," Pete said. "I really do. But what you're proposing is not a good idea." He turned to me. "Andy's talking about having Weiss stay with him in Newton and help him with the work on Chadwick Street."

"Interesting idea." I said.

Andy frowned. "Pete doesn't agree."

"Why not?" I asked. Pete was a pretty savvy guy. If he didn't like the idea, he would have a good reason.

"It's simple," Pete said. "We know nothing about this man. I say there's no point taking chances."

I gave that some serious thought. After what Tiffany had, or hadn't, learned about the man, it might be a good idea to keep an eye on him. "I think Andy should go for it. It'll save some major money, which is important. It'll get the job done sooner, so Andy can rent out all six apartments and earn some serious rent. It'll also give a break to someone who's down on his luck and could use some help. Besides, Andy will be there every day to keep tabs on the guy. So why not?"

Pete gave me a look which screamed "Have you lost your mind?"

I pretended not to notice. Any other thoughts I had on the subject I would keep to myself. Time would tell if it was a good idea or not.

Our meals arrived and we lapsed into companionable silence. Then Andy's phone rang. He grabbed it from his pocket and studied the display. "It's my tenant Ellen!" he said. "Finally! I'm going to step outside to take this." And off he dashed.

I was seriously enjoying my salmon when Andy returned. Collapsing into his chair, he held his head in his hands and sobbed.

"Good lord, Andy, what is it? Is Ellen all right?" I asked.

Pete squeezed Andy's shoulder. "It can't be as bad as all that. Tell us what she said."

Andy let out a sad and mighty sigh. "I'm sorry to say that it wasn't Ellen. It was a friend of hers. April something-or-other." His eyes filled up.

"And?" I asked. Based on the horrified look on Andy's face, I was almost afraid to hear what was coming next.

"She told me Ellen is dead." His voice was unsteady; his hands shook.

I dropped my fork. "That's awful, Andy. Dear God! What happened?"

"She OD'd. April blames that damn Florescu guy. She says he treated Ellen badly, knocked her around a lot. And that he seemed to have a diabolical hold over the girl. April suspects that Florescu gave Ellen some bad stuff, cocaine probably, or heroin. Maybe he even did it deliberately."

From what I'd heard and seen about Florescu, that seemed entirely possible.

I slipped into investigator mode, mostly in an effort to keep myself from losing it altogether. "Please tell me she reported this to the police."

Andy shook his head. "Nope. April doesn't want to get involved. She's scared that Florescu will come after her. I promised I'd leave her out of it." He dropped a wadded up napkin on the table. It had April's name and a telephone number written on it.

"Then you need to call the police," I told him. "Right now."

Andy frowned. "I don't know about that."

"What do you mean you don't know?" Pete asked. "Of course you need to call them."

"And tell them my tenant is dead? No way. They already suspect I had something to do with the fencer's death. And the baby as well, for all I know. And now there's a third unexplained death associated with my property. They'll lock me up and throw away the key."

"That isn't going to happen," Pete said. "Come on. I'll follow you home and we'll call them together. It'll be all right."

"Pete's right," I said. "You guys go do what you have to do. I'll settle things here. Hang in there, Andy." If I concentrated on handling the business end of things, it would help keep me my emotions in check. At least I hoped it would.

"Thanks, Ames," Pete said. "I'll call you later."

Snatching up the napkin with the girl's information on it, I mulled over this latest unsettling development, wondering how it fit in with the rest of Andy's ever-increasing problems. I needed to remain calm and think clearly. To figure out a way to get to the bottom of things – and hopefully not find Andy at the bottom when I got there. At the moment, I wasn't sure if I should be concerned about the guy or suspicious of him.

CHAPTER 22

I arrived at work the next morning in a better frame of mind. Per Pete's late night call, Andy was managing to hold it together. He had done well enough speaking with the police. They hadn't pushed him too hard or accused him of anything. They were now checking into recent unidentified female deaths in an attempt to locate Ellen James' body.

That was enough of a relief that I actually finished George's job review before calling it a day. I was satisfied with the result. I called him as soon as I was settled and asked him to see me in my office.

"What's up?" he snarled.

"I have something for you. I think you might like it." Maybe that would pique his curiosity enough to get him here right away.

It did.

"Here as requested," he said as he strolled in with an exaggerated nonchalance.

He didn't call me Hotshot, as he often did, but I knew he wanted to. I pasted a smile on my face and said, "Thanks for making time for me. I know how busy you are."

He probably knew I was making that up, but he had the good sense not to say so. Instead, he grunted, "Right. No problem."

"I have your annual review here. I thought we'd get it out of the way early. Then we can both get on with our day. And I wanted to be sure your raise went through on time."

His eyes lit up. "Raise? I wasn't sure there'd be raises this year. Difficult fiscal times and all that."

"We managed to find a little money for you."

The smug look on his face said, "I certainly deserve it." His mouth remained closed. Smart move.

"How does six percent sound to you?" I asked. "Three percent immediately and the rest upon completion of a few goals, thus, delayed but retroactive."

"Six percent sounds pretty good." He fidgeted in his seat, then asked, "What's this about goals? What kind of goals are we talking about?"

I took a deep breath and steeled myself to deliver the news to him handily, the good news as well as the bad. "Let me start by saying that your job performance is not an issue." That was the closest I could come to an honest compliment. "You are good at what you do." *Even though sometimes that includes throwing hissy fits. You're excellent at that as well.*

His eyebrows arched. "Uh, thanks. I do my best."

"Here's the deal: I am well aware that you don't care for training the people under your supervision. That's all right. We can deal with that in another way. But the issue is that you have skills and knowledge that need to be shared with others."

He cocked his head. "How do you propose we do that?"

"I propose that you put together a training manual consisting of all the things that are important but that you'd rather not be teaching. Assemble the information in a logical way and give it to Peggy. Not only does she love to train people, but she's also quite good at it. Your knowledge and her skills together will make a killer combination."

120

George was quiet for a few moments. I could almost see the wheels turning in his head. Finally, he said, "Hmmm, interesting. That might actually work."

That was probably the most positive response I'd get from the guy.

"Is there anything else?" he asked.

"There sure is." *Did you think I'd make it this easy for you?* "You know Michael Piscatelli from the third floor?"

"Mike? Of course I know him. He's a good guy. Why?" George fell silent, a small frown on his face. "Mike's been out lately, hasn't he?"

"Right. He had back surgery. Major back surgery. He'll be out for at least the next few months dealing with rehab. When he returns, it'll probably be part-time, at least for a while."

"And ...?"

"And I want you to help cover for him."

George's eyes grew wide. "Cover for him how?"

"Not to worry. I'm not asking you to assume all of Mike's responsibilities. Just some of them. Those that fit your skill set." I couldn't believe I'd actually used the term skill set. It was enough to make a person think I'd been drinking the corporate Kool Aid. "The rest of his duties will be parceled out to others so that nothing goes uncovered."

George looked skeptical, just sat there with his hands folded in his lap.

"I figured that once you put the training material together for Peggy, the time you used to spend doing the training yourself would be freed up. Helping out with Mike's work seemed to be a good way to fill up that time. When he's back full-time, we'll find something else for you. There's always a need somewhere."

He couldn't argue with that logic. "Is that all?"

"Not quite. There is one other thing."

"Oh?"

I worked hard at keeping a straight face as I told him, "I want you to attend the next available 'Service with a Smile' seminar. There's usually one in the area every few weeks." I held my breath, waiting to see if he'd explode at this idea. Or perhaps stomp out the door in a huff.

"You've got to be kidding. Sit through a couple days of that crap? But why? It's not like I do any actual customer service."

"I know that. However, I do believe the seminar will be beneficial to you in a number of ways. Most particularly, it will raise your awareness of the expectations placed on those who do provide service to our customers. It's a lot easier to work with people when you understand why they're doing what they're doing." *And just maybe it'll sweeten your foul disposition a bit in the process.*

He sat stone-faced for what seemed like forever. Then he said, "If I understand this correctly, if I do everything you've outlined here, I'll get a decent pay increase. If I don't, I'll get diddly squat."

I wasn't sure three percent was actually diddly squat, but I held my tongue. "You'll also eliminate your role in the training aspect of the job. Which will give you more time to spend on the duties you enjoy. Those things which you are quite good at. From where I sit, it's a win-win."

He closed his eyes and screwed up his face. Finally, he said, "You're right. OK. We've got a deal."

Whew!

I passed him his copy of the review and had him sign my copy.

"That's great. Please understand that there is a timeline involved here. I will expect you to begin fulfilling your end of the arrangement right away."

He frowned, but didn't argue. "Is there anything else?"

"No. We're all set here. Enjoy your day."

He rose and headed for the door. "You too. And, uh, well, thanks."

Thus ended the most civilized conversation George and I had had in a couple of years.

Peggy poked her head in as soon as George had left. "How'd it go?"

I gave her two thumbs up. "Piece of cake."

"Should be interesting to see how he handles things," she said.

I agreed. "Either he'll make it or he won't." And while I couldn't wait to see which outcome it would be, I'd be all right with either. I was happy this chore was over. Now I could get back to the parts of my job that I actually enjoyed. There was a lot I wanted to accomplish by the end of the day.

CHAPTER 23

I placed a call to Ted Rosen, the oh-so-very-dapper medical examiner I had met on Tuesday. He answered his own phone, which pleased me. I wasn't big on going through the circuitous channels of officialdom. An annoying waste of time.

"Of course I remember you," he said. "You're the lady with the lovely blue eyes I met the other morning on Chadwick Street. I met your dog as well. What can I do for you today?"

It was nice to be remembered. "I'm hoping you can tell me that you've completed the postmortems on both of the bodies found in that cellar and that you'd love to fill me in on all the gory details."

He laughed. "Postmortems are done, but I'm uncertain why I should be sharing my results with you."

"Because they're related to my investigation. It's not just the fire damage that concerns me. There's a serious liability issue. I need to determine whether or not there's a possibility our property owner could be held responsible for the fencer's before I can close the case."

He gave that some thought. "Do you believe your property owner was in any way responsible for Mr. Zupkoff's death?"

"What I believe is irrelevant. If the owner could be blamed for creating or allowing a situation which led to a death, NEC&I could be involved."

"Give me one good reason why," he said.

I replied, "I can give you a million good reasons."

"Please explain that."

"We write one million dollars liability coverage on the property. If the owner were held responsible for Howie Zupkoff's death, NEC&I could be on the line for a great deal of money."

"*Hmmmm.* You may just have a point there."

"And the police have been questioning Mr. Yesley, the property owner." I told him.

"Do they believe he was somehow involved in either the fire or the fencer's death?"

"They haven't shared their thoughts with me."

I could hear the wheels turning in his head. "I can't speak to the cause of the fire," he said. "That's outside of my job description. But I can assure you that Mr. Yesley did not murder Mr. Zupkoff."

"That's good news. What makes you say so?" I asked.

"The man wasn't murdered."

That was a shock. "What are you saying? Then how did he die? And why?"

"It's rather difficult to explain over the phone. Far easier to demonstrate. If you can come to my office, I will show you what I mean."

"You're willing to do that?"

"I realize we're pushing the envelope a bit here. Still, you have convinced me that your company could have a legitimate interest in the cause of death. And I like you. You remind me of my daughter. I also like your dog. Besides, I'll be retiring shortly. There's not much the powers that be can do to me if they disagree with my decision. When would you like to stop by?"

At the risk of being overly-assertive, I replied, "How busy are you right now?"

"Never too busy for a pretty woman. But we'll have to make it quick. I need to leave here no later than 11:30. I have a prior commitment."

"In that case, I'll be right there." I grabbed my briefcase and bolted out the door before he could change his mind. I called an uber. The chances of finding a parking space on Albany Street in Boston in the middle of a weekday morning were somewhere between slim and none. Some days I'm smarter than I am on others.

My ride deposited me in front of 720 Albany Street fifteen minutes later. Dr. Rosen met me at the door, looking every bit as well turned-out as he had the other day. The man was a fashion plate.

"Hello," I said. "Thanks for seeing me on such short notice."

The medical examiner's office was just before the entrance to the morgue, which pleased me no end. I had been dreading the thought of walking through there.

We settled in. I pulled out a pen and a notebook, eager to take notes on whatever he had discovered.

Rosen didn't waste time on idle chit-chat. "Let's begin with Howie Zupkoff. Poor kid. Far too young to die."

I agreed.

"It's obvious that the poor fellow bled to death. What's interesting, however, is how that came to be."

"I thought you had the murder weapon. Some kind of an axe, wasn't it?"

"Correct."

He donned a pair of gloves, then opened a closet behind his desk and pulled out a gardening tool with a wooden handle at least three or four feet long. I was guessing at the length. Never was very good at weights and measures. The tool was just as Jimmy Landry had described it to me. It resembled something between a large

126

toothpick and a small garden hoe. The business end had a long, pointed edge on one side and a shovel-like blade on the other.

"Here we have Exhibit A," Rosen said. "A simple tool used to break up hard-packed earth. A pick mattock, sometimes referred to as a San Angelo Bar. It is quite capable of doing some serious damage. The actual weapon is locked in the evidence room. This is an exact duplicate, right down to the pattern of the stains on the handle. On the actual weapon, the stains are blood. This is shoe polish." He held the tool out for my inspection.

I studied the tool and drew a likeness of it in my notebook. "I was informed it had been wiped clean of fingerprints." *Much to my chagrin.*

"You were told correctly. All we found was the victim's blood on the pick and bits of dirt from the cellar floor on the blade."

I gave this some thought. "That suggests that whoever was using this tool was digging in the cellar before killing Howie. My guess is that he was attempting to dig up the suitcase containing the baby's body."

Rosen nodded. "So it would appear. And that's where things become interesting."

I leaned forward in my chair. "In what way?"

"The late Mr. Zupkoff was tall, nearly six-foot three. What do you suppose that tells us about the attack on him?"

"That his attacker was also tall?"

"Perhaps, but not likely. I did a little research. Google is a marvelous tool. In the U.S. population, only fourteen percent of all men are six feet tall. And only just under four percent are over six foot two."

I waited for the punch line.

"Allow me to demonstrate something." Rosen held the pick mattock with the chisel point facing in my direction. "Please note that the stain is of even length all the way around."

I took a good look. He was right.

"And what does that tell us?" Rosen asked.

Only one thing made sense to me. "That the point entered the victim's body straight on, not at an angle."

"Correct," he said.

"But if the killer was shorter than the victim, how could that be?"

He smiled, apparently pleased with my response. "If you would be good enough to stand up, I can demonstrate."

I stood.

"I'm certainly not over six feet," he began, "but you're short enough that there is a significant difference in our heights." He handed me the pick mattock. "Grab this by the handle and attempt to come at me with it, though gently, please. No actual contact."

I futzed around with the tool, trying to devise a way to have the chisel point stab him straight on. There was no way. "I get what you're saying. I'm just not sure what it means."

A big Ta Da smile graced his face. "I believe it means we are looking at an accident here, not a deliberate murder."

Interesting idea. I couldn't wait to hear how he arrived at this conclusion.

"Turn around," Rosen instructed me, "and make like you're digging in the dirt, using the shovel end of the tool."

I did as instructed.

"Bear in mind that the dirt floor is hard-packed, and probably partially frozen as well. You raise your tool over your head to hit the floor with additional force. Now imagine me coming up behind you silently at that very moment."

I attempted this maneuver, curious to see where it would lead.

"Now keep your arms up where they are but turn your head in my direction. And note where the point of the tool is in relation to my body."

Holy shit! If I had used a bit more force, the point would have gone straight into the medical examiner's chest.

"Good Lord. How did you figure that out?"

He grinned. "Simple kinetics. Combined with a modicum of imagination."

I was impressed. "And it means that Mr. Zupkoff's death was accidental."

"So it would seem. And once the killer realized what he had done, he wiped his tool clean of any fingerprints."

Wow! I wasn't sure what any of this had to do with the fire, not yet, anyway. But I was convinced that somehow it all fit together. "What about the baby?" I asked. "Were you able to learn anything about him, or her?"

Rosen shook his head. "Sadly, no. Not even the gender. Too much time has elapsed. Too much deterioration. We'll probably never know what happened to the poor little thing."

That made me sad. "What about DNA? Could you learn something from that?"

"But what could we learn? Without a sample to compare it to, such a test would be pointless. Not to mention time-consuming and costly."

Bummer. "Did you check the suitcase for fingerprints?"

He smiled. "We did. It was covered with them. I sent them along to Detective Donnelly to see if he can find a match."

I had a thought, perhaps even a brainstorm. "What if you also check the pick-axe for DNA?"

"Interesting idea. I'll run it by Donnelly. DNA tests require his official blessing."

Rosen's cell phone rang. He glanced at the caller ID. "Sorry, I have to take this." He stepped into the hallway before saying hello,

I sat and used the time to make some notes.

Rosen returned a few moments later. "I have a favor to ask of you."

I sat up at attention.

"Speak of the devil, that was Detective Donnelly on the phone, looking for my findings on Mr. Zupkoff. I told him exactly what I told you earlier. It requires a demonstration. The problem is that he wants it today. I'm scheduled to present a seminar at U Mass Boston in less than thirty minutes. I'll be tied up all afternoon."

I sat patiently, listening to all this, unsure of where he was going.

"I told Donnelly I'd send someone else over to demonstrate my findings for him. If you would be so kind."

"You want me to do it?"

"Indeed I do. He's expecting you at 3:00. though I didn't tell him it was you."

I broke into a silly grin. "I'd be delighted to stand in for you, Dr. Rosen." *Some days you just get lucky.*

Duplicate pick mattock in hand, I thanked Dr. Rosen and called an uber, looking forward to 3:00 and eager to see the look on Detective Donnelly's face when I arrived.

CHAPTER 24

Back at the office, I phoned Ursula Fagan, Andy's tenant who was now staying at her daughter's home in Quincy. The phone rang six times before she picked up. At that point, I was expecting voicemail. A live voice was nice. I identified myself, then asked, "Would it be possible for me to visit with you today? I have a few questions about your old neighborhood in Dorchester."

"Of course, Dear," she said. "I'd be happy to tell you anything I can. Why don't you plan on arriving after lunchtime? We can have some tea and a nice chat. But tell me, why do you want to talk about Morton Street? It was so very long ago that I lived there."

"Actually, I'm interested in your Chadwick Street neighborhood."

She let out a little laugh. "Of course you are. How silly of me. All right then. I'll see you after lunch."

That settled, I spent some time catching Peggy up on the latest developments. Also thanking her for holding down the fort while I was out and about.

"This case gets more interesting by the day," she said. "I can't wait for the next installment. Oh, by the way, I heard you and George had an interesting conversation this morning."

"News travels fast. How did you come by that tidbit?"

"From the man himself. He stopped by a while ago to let me know he'd have his training information ready for me in a few days. He seems quite pleased with the arrangement. It's as if he thinks he got promoted."

"That's all right. Let him strut a bit. Maybe he'll be pleased enough to call a truce between the two of us." *One can always hope.*

Peggy rolled her eyes. "From your lips to God's ears. What are you up to for the rest of the day?"

"I'll have a quick lunch then head out again. There's lots to do. Places to go, people to see, mysteries to solve, bad guys to catch. I'm going to Quincy then Dorchester. After that, I need to pay a visit to Detective Donnelly. Luckily, he works out of the Hancock Street location in Dorchester. It's a lot more convenient than downtown Boston. I may or may not make it back here today. It's too soon to tell."

"Shall I call you an uber?"

"No thanks. I'll walk home and grab my car. Maybe take Sam for a quick walk. He could use some air. It's an easy drive to Quincy this time of day. And there's reasonable parking where I'm going, so that shouldn't be a problem." And I never got tired of driving my Mustang. Even in the dead of winter, when I couldn't put the top down. Even when I was only heading down to Ursula Fagan's current residence in Quincy, just south of Boston.

The neighborhood was old but well-kept. Mostly multi-families with screened-in front porches and small yards. Ursula's daughter's house was a typical two-family wood-frame building, similar to Andy's property, only smaller. It was neat and tidy, painted beige with pale blue trim. A statue of Our Lady of Lourdes stood in the shrubbery by the front door. Mary on the Half Shell.

I rang the bell for the first floor apartment. It was a few moments before Ursula arrived at the door. She had a head full of chalk-white curls, blue eyes and a warm smile. "Come in, Dear," she greeted me. "Sorry it took me so long to get here. This walker sure does slow me down."

"Not to worry. I'm just happy you have time to speak with me." Limited mobility must suck. I handed her my card.

She studied it for a moment, then said, "I'm sorry, Dear, but I really don't think I need any more insurance."

My hopes for some useful information began to fade. "Actually I'm here to speak with you about your home on Chadwick Street."

She frowned ever so slightly. "Of course you are. I remember now. Please don't stand out there in the cold. Come into the kitchen and I'll make you a nice cup of hot tea. It'll take the chill off."

"This is a lovely place," I said as she set the kettle to boil.

"My daughter Maggie did a nice job with it," Ursula said. "At first, I was horrified when she and her husband moved here from Dorchester, but I have grown to like the place. It's a nice location, walkable to the shops downtown, to the T station and to the beach. For those that can get around, that is. I don't get out much anymore."

"Did you always live in Dorchester? Until the fire, that is."

"Indeed I did. I was born on Morton Street. In St. Brendan's Parish."

I smiled at her use of the local idiom. Dorchester residents always referred to the parish where they lived rather than the neighborhood.

"We lived in a two-family house my mother's cousin owned," she continued. "My parents never dared to try to buy a place of their own, or to rent from a stranger."

"Why was that?"

"They were here illegally," she said. "Back then a lot of folks were."

I remembered having heard that, once upon a time, the largest illegal immigrant population in Boston was the Irish.

"When did you move to Chadwick Street?" I asked.

"When I got married. It was a nice neighborhood. Will and I had a good life there. Then he died of a heart attack. He was young, only in his forties. Life was never the same after that, but I didn't want to move. I was comfortable where I was. People looked out for each other. It helped me get through a difficult time. Kept me from missing Will too much. I had good friends there. Nice memories." She set two cups of tea on the kitchen table, along with a plate of obviously home-made cookies.

They smelled divine.

"That's actually what I'd like to ask you about," I said. "Your neighbors."

"The lady next door and I were great friends for years. We had wonderful times together. Her name was Helen something-or-other."

"Helen Czwakiel?"

Ursula smiled. "Right. That's it. Czwakiel. How could I forget a name like that?"

"I'm interested in your neighbors at 12 Chadwick Street. Did you know everybody who lived in the building?"

"Sure did. Many of us lived there for years. Good folks, mostly."

It would be interesting to learn what 'mostly' meant. "I'm particularly curious about people who lived there around twenty years ago. Was there somebody with a baby?"

Ursula closed her eyes for a moment then smiled. "Yes. Of course. The Grants had a baby. A little boy. Cute as pie he was. Named Timmy, if I remember correctly."

"Were there any other babies in the house back then?"

Ursula thought for a moment. "No. Not that I can recall."

I worked at maintaining a calm exterior. Inside I was jumping for joy and trying not to jump to conclusions. Ursula might just help me unravel the mystery of the baby in the cellar. And it would be nice to put a name to the poor little baby. I'd figure out a way to confirm it somehow. "Were you friendly with the Grants?"

"With Marissa, yes. She was a lovely girl. The two of us would walk the baby around the neighborhood in his pram on fine days. We got to know each other well. Sometimes I'd babysit so she and her husband could go out." She frowned. "I didn't much like him though. Richard was his name. Jesus, Mary and Joseph, that man was a bully and a brute. I hated the way he spoke to Marissa. He didn't treat her well at all. Too many times I heard them arguing at night. He'd yell. She'd cry. A lot. No, I had little use for that man."

I made notes while Ursula came up for air.

"And the way he treated that poor wee child," she continued. "Mother of God, it was shameful. Both Dick and Marissa worked funny hours. Sometimes she had to leave the baby with him while she went to work. Some father he was. I'd see him sitting on his porch drinking beer while that poor child was howling like a banshee. You'd think the man was stone deaf. Though he was probably drunk. He was a selfish boor, not to mention a terrible father."

"Did they live there long?"

"A couple of years. They weren't married when they first moved in. Back then that was a big scandal. But I figured it was none of my business. They got married after a year or so. Then one day I woke up to learn that Marissa was gone. She and the baby had moved out and left that lout of a man. He spent a lot of time in that nasty cellar after she left. Lord knows what he was doing down there. Such an odd man."

I shuddered, wondering if he was in the cellar to bury the baby. I wasn't going to burden Ursula with that question. There was no point. "Did you ever hear from Marissa?"

Ursula nodded. "Yes. A few months later, I got a letter from her. She said she couldn't live with Richard and his temper any longer. She was beginning to fear for her life. She'd moved back home and begun using her maiden name."

"Did she tell you how the baby was doing?"

A dark cloud passed over Ursula's face. "Come to think of it, she didn't mention him at all. That's strange, isn't it?"

Maybe not so strange. "Do you remember where her home was?" Tracking Marissa down could answer a lot of the questions floating around in my head.

Ursula shook her head. "Not off-hand, but I did save her letter. It's in my keepsake box. My daughter Maggie brought it to me last week when I got out of the hospital. Maggie worries about me living alone. She insisted I spend at least a few days with her. She was over at Chadwick Street to get a few of my things. The keepsake box was on the list I gave her. I have it in the other room. Shall we look for the letter?" She lifted herself up into her walker. "You wait here. I'll be right back."

That was a stroke of luck. Some days you just live right. I munched on a chocolate chip cookie while I waited for Ursula to return. She was gone a while, long enough for three cookies.

"Sorry about the wait," she said as she re-seated herself and opened the painted wooden box. "It took me a minute to remember where I'd put the box." She handed me a faded old envelope. "The postmark says Lee, Massachusetts. Do you know where that is?"

"Western Mass.," I said. "In the Berkshires. I believe it's not far from Stockbridge. You know, where Alice's Restaurant was."

She gave me a funny look. Maybe she wasn't an Arlo Guthrie fan. "Yes. Now I remember. She told me she was from the westernmost part of the state, almost into New York."

I took another look at the envelope. There was no return address. "Do you know what Marissa's maiden name was?" With any luck maybe she still lived in Lee.

Ursula shook her head. "Nope. Sorry."

I frowned, frustrated to be at a dead end.

"Wait a minute!" Ursula grinned. "I know where I can find her maiden name. And it's right here in this box."

"What do you mean?"

"It's her wedding invitation. I saved it because it was so pretty. And I didn't get invited to a lot of weddings in those days. Theirs was at St. Brendan's church, with a lovely reception downstairs in the parish hall. It was a nice party. Big feed. Lively music. Dancing." Ursula smiled as she handed me the invitation. "After such a lovely wedding, it's a shame things didn't work out better for the two of them."

I examined the invitation. Marissa Albert. With a name and a town, I might just be able to locate the woman.

"What became of Richard after Marissa left?"

Ursula rolled her eyes. "He moved out a few months later. God knows where he went. My guess is the man came to a bad end. Even on his best day, he was odd as two Hells."

I had just one final question. "How well do you know the current tenants?"

"Not well at all, really. That fellow Weiss has only been there for a few months. October, I think it was, when he moved in. I was in the hospital at the time, then in rehab for six weeks. I never actually met the man, just saw him from a distance or heard him on the stairs. He seemed quiet, kept to himself. Ellen, the other tenant, was always pleasant enough when that boyfriend of hers wasn't around. I don't think he actually lived there, but he was around a lot. He wasn't nice." A frown dashed across Ursula's face. "Come to think of it, he treated that poor girl much the same way that Richard treated Marissa. That's odd, isn't it?"

Odd, perhaps, but not terribly helpful. Time to go. "Mrs. Fagan, you can't believe how important this information is to my investigation. I can't thank you enough."

She beamed. "Glad I was able to help. I always liked Marissa."

My head was spinning from my conversation with Ursula. My heart ached for the baby buried in that cellar all these years, cold and alone. Could it be Timmy Grant? I needed to process that, along with everything else Ursula had told me. And the best place to do that was at the beach.

I drove to the end of Elm Avenue and turned onto Quincy Shore Drive. Even in January, the sight of the ocean had a wonderful effect on me. It could calm and energize me, both at the same time. It helped me think.

Pulling into a parking lot facing the beach, I opened the window and closed my eyes. Time to let things float around inside my head.

One thing I suspected was that Richard Grant may have killed his infant son and buried him in the cellar. Based on what I'd just learned, it wasn't that much of a leap. How that connected to the fire on Chadwick Street and to Howie Zupkoff's death was something else entirely. Technically, my only interest here was the fire, but I couldn't let go of the rest of it. Timmy Grant, or whoever that baby was, deserved a decent burial.

I did a mental review of everything I knew about the house on Chadwick Street – both past and present – beginning with who had lived there twenty years ago, then who lived there now. I mulled over everything Peggy and Tiffany had discovered about the current tenants, as well as everything I knew about the neighbors. I listened to the roar of the ocean, breathed in the salt air and waited for all my random thoughts to coalesce.

Then they did. It hit me like a lightning bolt. I didn't need to think about it for long. I had an idea, and a plan, and just about enough time to pull it off.

I telephoned Peggy from the car and repeated what I'd learned from Ursula. "Can you do your magic with the Registry, Facebook, Google, and whatever else to see what you can learn about Marissa Albert? She's probably living in the Berkshires. Concentrate on that."

"Piece of cake."

Thank goodness Peggy felt that way. A confirmed technophobe, I had no patience with computer searches. And I needed to locate the woman to learn what had happened to her baby. If the child buried in the cellar was her Timmy, she deserved to know he'd been found.

CHAPTER 25

I needed to make a quick trip to Chadwick Street to check out a few things. I was curious to see how the work was progressing. ServPro was supposed to be starting on the second floor today. And Douglas Weiss was working with Andy. There was one thing in particular I wanted to check on, and this was the perfect opportunity.

I pulled into a Dunkin' on Hancock Street and purchased a dozen donuts and six cups of coffee. I got the coffees all black, then grabbed several little creamers and a handful of sugars. You never knew how people took their coffee. Better to be prepared. It was mid-afternoon. The guys would be ready for a pick-me-up.

The ServPro truck was in front of the house. I parked my Mustang a little way up the street and walked back, Dunkin' bags in my hands. Andy and Weiss were in the side yard working on replacing the cellar widows.

"Hi guys," I called to them.

They stopped what they were doing and walked over to me. Andy pointed to the bags I was carrying. "Are those for us?"

I grinned. "I figured you guys would be ready for a break."

"Sure are," Andy said as we walked toward the house.

We entered through the opening where the front door belonged. A large piece of plywood stood off to one side.

"The new door is on back-order," Andy told me. "Something about it being an unusual size. They'll deliver it in a few days. In the meantime, I've got to put the plywood back up at the end of every day. What a nuisance."

We climbed the stairs to the second floor. The ServPro team was hard at work in the vacant apartment on the left, all dressed up in safety goggles and heavy-duty gloves. Drop cloths covered the floors. There were several industrial size spray bottles of Febreze Air Freshener. Good idea. The building still reeked of smoke.

The apartment was freezing. I shivered, then noticed that every window was wide open.

"Sorry about the temperature," Andy said. "We need to air the house out big time. At the very least, it helps to mitigate that dreadful odor."

I shivered again and said, "Anything that does the trick is fine with me." But I would definitely keep my coat on.

"Not only that," Andy said, "but the ServPro guys tell me that smoke fumes and cleaning products can irritate your lungs. I'm not taking any chances with that."

In all the years I'd sent ServPro out to clean up after fire losses, I had never actually seen them at work. From the way they moved about, it was obvious they had the process down to a science. One of them, the tallest, was vacuuming the ceilings and walls with some oversized and very noisy equipment. As he completed an area, the other two workers washed it down with soapy water and the largest sponges I had ever seen.

"I thought you folks could use a treat," I told them. And perhaps a few minutes of relative quiet. That machine was deafening.

The tall fellow smiled. "Well aren't you nice? Sounds great. OK, guys. Time for a break."

The others stopped what they were doing and grinned in my direction. "Yes, Boss," they said in unison. "Sounds good."

Andy found a small table and a few mismatched chairs in the other second floor apartment, which was currently unoccupied. We set the coffee and donuts up in there. Not luxurious, but at least a tad warmer than where they'd been working.

Andy made the introductions. The tall guy shook my hand.

I distributed the coffee. Everybody except Weiss added cream. Andy and the ServPro boss used two sugars each. All five men attacked the donuts with gusto. I sat back and nibbled on a jelly stick. It was a little tricky to do with wool gloves on, but I was damned if I'd take them off. The ServPro guys were apparently made of tougher stuff than I was. They all removed their big heavy gloves.

As we snacked, I made small talk with them – the weather, where they lived, the Celtics. They were chatty guys. Andy didn't add much to the conversation. Weiss never said a word.

"How long do you expect this job to take?" I asked them.

The tall fellow answered, "A couple of days. It all depends on how bad the smoke damage is in the upper floor and in the cellar, once we can get in down there."

Thinking of the cellar gave me an idea. I turned to Andy and told a bold-faced lie. "I almost forgot. The police want you to seal the cellar up tight until they're able to complete their crime scene investigation. They say you should lock all the windows, bolt the bulkhead and the rear door and nail the inside door to the cellar shut. They don't expect to get back here until some time next Tuesday."

Andy accepted this as fact. "I'll get on it right away."

Then it was time to bring Weiss into the conversation. "Have you moved in with Andy yet?"

He smiled. "First thing this morning. I can't tell you how happy I am to be there, how grateful I am to Andy for helping me out at such a difficult time in my life. There was no way I could afford to stay at that motel any longer."

I remained silent, curious to see if he had anything else on his mind.

He did. "I'm only working part-time right now. I'll have plenty of time to help Andy here" he said. "I need to start looking for a full-time job soon though. The trouble is that nobody will give me the time of day if I don't have a permanent address. In the meantime, I'm happy to do what I can to help Andy. He's been good to me."

"What kind of work do you do?" I asked.

"Carpentry. Remodeling. Anything related to construction."

That was a relief. He was actually qualified to help Andy. "Are you a union carpenter?"

He shook his head, "Nope. I've always preferred my independence."

I could relate to that. "Which apartment is yours?"

"Third floor on the right. I can't wait to move back in."

"Time to get back to work, guys," the ServPro boss said. Turning to me, he added, "Thanks for the treats."

They all rose and began to clear their trash.

"Let me do that," I told them as I grabbed the empty coffee cups. "You fellows have enough to do." I bagged the trash carefully and prepared to leave.

"You can dump that stuff here," Andy said, pointing to a grimy barrel in the hallway.

"That's OK. I've got this," I said. Then I was out the door and on my way before he could question this decision or ask me why it mattered. Which it did.

CHAPTER 26

It was a short ride from Chadwick Street to the Boston Police Headquarters on Hancock Street in Dorchester. I didn't give my name at the front desk, but simply identified myself as coming from Dr. Rosen's office to see Detective Donnelly.

Donnelly looked up from his desk at the sound of my knock. "Ms. Lynch, I'm afraid I have no time for you today. I'm expecting someone any minute now."

I flashed him my best smile. "That would be me." I held the substitute pick mattock up for him as proof.

He jumped up from his chair. "Excuse me? Rosen sent you? What the Hell's going on?"

I plunked myself into his visitor's chair. "I was in Dr. Rosen's office when you called. He had just finished his demonstration for me. Since he was tied up and I knew what you needed to see, he asked me to come here in his stead."

Donnelly rolled his eyes. "You do realize that you're not an actual employee of either the Boston Police Department or the medical examiner's office?"

I fought back a grin. "Of course I do. But bear in mind, I was asked to help out today. Perhaps you could think of me as a concerned

143

citizen who may actually have information vital to your case." *And if you're not nice to me, I might not share it all with you.*

He sat back in his chair and stared at the ceiling. "Well, as long as you're here, let's get this over with. You know, it's a good thing you're cute. It's the only thing that keeps me from booting you out."

And I was glad it did. I filled him in on the conversation I'd had with the medical examiner, complete with a live demonstration of how the stabbing had probably happened. And a fine job I did of it, if I did say so myself.

Donnelly watched my re-enactment in bemused silence, then appeared to be mulling things over. "Interesting. And if Rosen says that's how it happened, who am I to disagree? He's a sharp guy. Knows what he's doing."

"He certainly made it sound convincing to me," I said.

Donnelly scratched his head. "It seems that you're involved in this whether I like it or not. So let's talk. What do Rosen's findings tell us about Mr. Zupkoff's death?"

That was easy. "It was an accident. A very sad accident. And I believe it's connected to the baby's body. It has to be."

"That would be one Hell of a connection," he said. "Especially given a gap in time over twenty years. But why was anybody digging up the baby's body now? I mean, really, how could all this fit together?"

"I'm working on that. I'll let you know when I figure it out."

"You mean if."

"No. I mean when." I didn't bother telling him about my bet with Pete, which I fully intended to win. "Bear in mind, Detective, that there is no such thing as a coincidence."

"What about the fire?" he asked. "Was that part of whatever was going on there as well? Are you thinking it was deliberately set?"

"The jury's still out on that. But my gut is telling me that it was accidental as well."

He gave me a big "gotcha" grin. "Wouldn't that make it a coincidence?"

I allowed him to gloat for a moment, then asked, "While we're on the subject, Andy Yesley tells me you questioned him intensely about the fire. You don't actually suspect the man, do you?"

"Just doing my job," Donnelly shrugged.

Perhaps a bit too aggressively. Or maybe not. I still wasn't sure what I thought about Andy. "Did you run the fingerprints on the suitcase?"

Donnelly glared at me. "I don't know why I should tell you any of this, since it's truly none of your business, but yes I did."

Aha! I knew I'd been growing on him. "And …? Did you get a hit?"

"Really Ms. Lynch. My understanding is that your role in this matter consists of investigating the fire, paying the insurance claim and, one time only, relaying information to me from the medical examiner."

The man was right of course, but I wasn't about to let that stop me. "I'll make a deal with you. How about we trade information? You show me yours, I'll show you mine."

Donnelly frowned. "This is not 'Let's Make a Deal.' And the Boston Police Department is not in the habit of exchanging information with ordinary citizens."

I suspected that was not exactly true, but chose to let it slide. I also resented him calling me ordinary. "How about this: I'll give you a name, and you tell me if it's the name associated with the prints you ran."

"I guess that couldn't hurt." He sat back and waited. "Shoot. I'm all ears."

"Richard Grant," I announced.

Donnelly's eyes grew wide. "How the Hell did you know that? What are you, some kind of witch or something?"

Hot damn! I was right. I gave him an unabbreviated account of my conversation with Ursula Fagan.

He took notes as I spoke, then said, "You really need to get yourself a different hobby, you know that?"

I grinned. "What can I say? Tell me, what do you know about Richard Grant?"

"The prints are definitely his. He has a criminal record. Showed up on our radar fifteen years ago. Lived in the house at 12 Chadwick Street. He got into a fight with a guy in a bar in Southie. Things got ugly. The guy died. Grant did fifteen years in Walpole for manslaughter. It should have been less time, but he kept messing up. Got paroled just over five months ago. Are you happy now?"

"Deliriously."

"Good. Thanks for your help, on this one and only occasion. Let's not make a habit of it."

You're welcome. I placed the Dunkin' bag on his desk and rummaged through it.

"Did you bring me coffee?" he asked.

"No. Sorry. I brought you trash." I continued going through the bag until I found what I was looking for.

"What kind of trash?"

"This kind." I placed a dirty coffee cup on Donnelly's desk. "I have a small favor to ask of you. I'm hoping you can check this cup for prints. It could be important."

He scowled. "Ms. Lynch, the Boston Police Department is not in the habit of checking trash for prints at the request of a member of the public. That's not how we operate."

I put on my oh-so-very-contrite face. "I do know that, Detective. Couldn't we just call this a professional courtesy? After all, I did provide you with information you wouldn't otherwise have."

"You've got me there." He knit his brows. "You're lucky I like you. All right. I'll run the damn prints. Just to humor you."

"Thanks. I appreciate it."

He eyed me suspiciously. "Would you care to tell me how you obtained these prints?"

I shook my head. "Could you also check the murder, or is it manslaughter, weapon for DNA?"

He rubbed his chin. "You think you're onto something, don't you?"

"I'm pretty sure I am."

"Care to share it?"

"Not just yet. First I need to get a few more ducks in a row. What do you think about the DNA?"

"I've got to give that some thought. Not sure I can justify it."

"I'm sure you can," I told him. "And when the results come in, you'll be glad you did."

I left him on that note, hoping his curiosity was sufficiently piqued.

CHAPTER 27

The thing I've always disliked the most about winter is the early sunsets. I could deal better with the snow and the cold if only there were a few more hours of sunlight each day. Apparently I run on solar energy. And if I don't get out of the office during the day, the light deprivation makes me cranky. I'd been outside plenty on this particular day, yet was cranky anyway. Go figure.

I went straight home from Donnelly's office, changed into jeans and a warm sweater and set out for a walk with Sam. No need for a flashlight; my neighborhood was well-lit. I did, however, grab my pepper spray on my way out the door. As safe as I felt in the area, I still wasn't taking any chances. My self-defense teacher said if you always bring the pepper spray with you, you won't ever need it. I chose to believe him.

He also said never to use your phone while walking at night. I was less conscientious about following that rule. I brought my cell with me tonight, , just in case it rang. I was hoping to hear from my parents. I needed to know they had arrived safely in Florida. On this rarest of occasions, I got my wish. The phone rang. It was my parents.

"It's about time you called," I scolded them. "I've been waiting for the news that you arrived safely and are all settled in."

"The phone does work both ways," Mom reminded me. She was good at things like that.

Guilty as charged. She often made me feel guilty of something or other. "I actually meant to call the other day," I said. "Then my week went crazy." It wasn't exactly a lie. "How was the drive down? Not too much for you folks?"

"Of course not," Dad bristled. "Everything went smoothly. We're not dead yet, you know."

Good to hear. "And how is Betsy?" I felt a twinge of guilt as I asked the question. While my older sister and I had never been close, I did need to put more effort into keeping in touch with her.

"Oh, you know your sister," my mother said. "Doing just fine. She loves being a wife and mother. She has a nice quiet life with Mike and the kids."

Mom's tone of voice said everything she didn't dare express aloud, "Why can't you be more like your sister? Are you ever going to give up this crazy life of yours and settle down with a nice guy?"

We'd had that conversation before. We would have it again. But not tonight. Instead, I asked "Is everything fine in Delray Beach?"

"Fine and then some," Dad chimed in. "It's not exactly beach weather yet, but very pleasant. Warm enough to spend time outside. We've begun taking long, lovely walks."

That was good news. Since my father retired, I'd been concerned he might not find enough to keep himself busy, let alone amused. He'd always been a workaholic.

"And there's always golf," I said.

My father laughed. "Would you believe that your mother has begun taking lessons? Before long, we'll be out on the course together."

"Good for you, Mom. Way to go." It was nice to see her willing to try something new.

"We might actually be able to make up a foursome," Mom said.

"Oh? Have you made some new friends?" I had been hoping they would. They'd only begun wintering in Delray Beach last year and hadn't met a lot of people yet.

"More like found some old friends," Dad said. "Do you remember Will Granger?"

"Your friend from Suffolk Law School?"

"Right."

"You two have been buddies forever. Is he down there?"

"At least for the time being," Mom said. "He and his wife Grace are looking for a place to buy. Hopefully in either Delray or Boynton Beach. It'd be nice to have them around. Such a pleasant couple. I always enjoyed them. And Grace is also thinking about taking up golf."

"Does that mean that Will is planning to retire?" I asked.

"He's working on it," Dad said. "As soon as he sells both his law practice and his home in Walpole."

Hmmmm. Very interesting. "Is the law practice in Walpole as well?"

"It is."

"What kind of law?"

"General practice. The usual small town stuff. Why do you ask?"

"No reason," I told him. That wasn't true. I had something in mind but wanted to give it more thought before saying anything. "I better get off the phone now, though. Sam and I are out walking and I need to pay attention. Stay well. I'll talk with you soon." I pocketed the phone.

Sam and I followed our usual nighttime three-block loop. He sniffed and snooped and did his business as I caught him up on the goings-on in my life. As always, he listened well, but didn't have many comments.

Then Sam's back stiffened. He let out a soft yet angry growl.

"What is it, Buddy?" As I turned my head to speak with him, I answered my own question. Somebody was across the street from us, strolling along and whistling softly. He wore jeans and a dark hoodie. Sam didn't like him.

I told myself it was simply a neighbor out for an evening stroll – nothing to worry about – but decided to test my theory, just in case. There was a cross street a few yards up ahead. I made an abrupt right turn onto it.

Sam availed himself of the chance to sniff out unfamiliar territory. That slowed us down. A chill ran up my spine as I heard the same soft whistling across the street. I snuck a peak, then shuddered. Our hooded friend had turned as well. He was still with us. And gaining ground.

Sam growled again. I shushed him and quickened our pace – not enough to be obvious, but hopefully enough to increase our distance from the whistler. I retrieved the pepper spray from my pocket and struggled to concoct a plan. As I turned onto Otis Street and headed toward my building, it came to me.

The dumpster!

My landlord had recently upgraded the area behind the building, hoping to prevent non-residents from leaving their trash there. He'd put up a chain-link fence around both the dumpster and the recycling bin and added a combination lock. If I could get there quickly enough, and punch in the access code, I could lock my pursuer out. And lock myself and Sam in. Not ideal, but it would buy me time to figure out my next move.

Breaking into a near-run, I dragged Sam with me to the gate. My hands shook as I entered the access code. It unlocked on the third try. Sam and I slipped inside then slammed the gate behind us. I nearly wept with relief, but decided to be angry instead. No way I'd let a creep in a hoodie make me cry. And Sam and I were safe.

We were also behind my building, on a cold, dark night, surrounded by trash. I stood in the shadows and peered through the fence. My hooded friend was nowhere to be seen. Sam continued to growl, though. I listened as the sound of whistling faded away.

Then I dialed 911.

Sam stopped growling and my hands stopped shaking when the police escorted us into the apartment.

"Are you sure you'll be all right, Ma'am?" one of the officers asked me.

"Yes. Of course. I'm fine." Truth be told, I wasn't fine, but had every intention of being so any minute now.

"And you have no idea who was following you?"

"Sorry." I actually had an idea, but I couldn't be right. At least I thought not. I thanked the officers, wished them well and bolted the door behind them.

Then I called Pete.

"Hello, my love," he said. "How are you?"

"Fine."

"What's wrong?"

"What makes you think anything is wrong?"

"I can tell by the sound of your voice. Has something happened?"

I gave him a quick run-down of my walk with Sam, trying to sound calm and casual about it. It didn't work.

"What were you and Sam doing out in the dark?"

I could hear the frown on his face. "Living our lives." *And we will continue to do so.*

"I get that, Ames," he said. "I really do. But you need to understand that I worry about you. A lot. Please tell me that you at least had your pepper spray with you."

"Always." That was a slight exaggeration, not exactly a lie.

"That's a relief, particularly now."

Uh oh. "Why? What do you mean?"

"I just saw on the news that Charlie Florescu is out of jail and on the run. He was being transferred to a more secure facility when he somehow disabled his guards and took off into the darkness. The guy must be like Houdini to get out of handcuffs. There's an APB out on him. I was worried he might end up in your neighborhood and try to harm you."

I thought that over. "I wondered if it might be him following me, then convinced myself it couldn't be. The guy was in jail. Or so I thought. Anyway, he couldn't possibly know where I live, or even my name."

"You sure?"

"Pretty sure, yeah. When I saw him yesterday on Chadwick Street, he only knew me as 'that bitch'. It'd be hard to track me down with nothing but that."

"How dare he refer to the love of my life in such a manner?"

That was my Pete. Forever ready to defend my honor.

"And yet it appears he managed to find you," Pete continued. "Probably furious about losing his cash and drugs from his girlfriend's apartment and somehow blaming you."

"But that still wouldn't explain how he found me."

"The important thing is that he did," Pete said. "Do you want me to come over this evening in case you need some protection?"

"I thought you were going to the fencing club."

"That was the plan. But I'm happy to change it for you. And I don't think you should be alone right now."

He was right about that. "Could you pick up some take-out on the way? My fridge is looking rather bare."

"Not a problem."

Thirty minutes later, Pete was at my door with Chinese food and not one, but two bottles of my favorite Sauvignon Blanc. He comforted me, I sobbed a bit, then we sat down to eat.

"How did your day go?" I asked between bites.

"It was a rotten combination of boring and annoying, but I managed to survive it."

"Things not so great at the office?"

"Could be better. I don't know how much longer I can deal with it."

From the sound of his voice, I'd guess not too long. Poor guy. Life is tough when you hate your job. I needed to do something to cheer him up. And suddenly I knew the very thing.

"What are you doing this weekend?" I asked.

"Spending it with you one way or another."

"Would you be interested in a road trip?"

"To where?" he asked.

"Anywhere. It doesn't matter. We both just need to get away. To be alone together. To relax. Have some fun. We could leave early Saturday morning, drive to somewhere nice, have a lovely dinner, spend the night somewhere charming and come back late on Sunday. What do you say?"

"OK. It's a deal. Sounds like fun."

"Great. We can discuss the details tomorrow. Figure out where we want to go."

That settled for the moment, I braced myself to broach a different subject with Pete, and it was making me uncomfortable. "There's something I need to ask you," I said, "and I don't think you're going to like it."

"What could you possibly ask that I wouldn't like?" He eyed me curiously.

I squirmed. "It's about Andy."

"What about him?"

"I've seen a lot of him lately. And I know he's going through a really tough time right now. I'm sure it's all very upsetting for him…," I hesitated.

"But?"

"But I'm beginning to wonder about his emotional reactions. They're almost a bit over the top. And I can't help but wonder …," I struggled with what to say next.

Pete saved me the trouble. "You wonder if his reactions are genuine – and that he truly is a big cry-baby – or if it's all a put-on to deflect suspicion from himself."

My entire body relaxed. "Well put. That's it exactly. My guess is that the police are wondering the same thing. They grilled him pretty intensely yesterday."

"I heard. And it really upset him."

"Pete, I know he's your cousin and you love him, but do you think there's any chance he is somehow involved in this mess?"

Pete took my hand. "And you've been hesitant to bring up the question, right?"

"That's for sure."

He smiled. "Believe it or not, the same thing crossed my mind as well. I have given it a good deal of thought."

"And?"

"And I think not. I've known Andy all his life. He was always hyper-sensitive, particularly as a kid. I used to try to toughen him up."

"Didn't work, did it?"

Pete shook his head. "Bottom line, Andy isn't up to anything wrong. He is just a big cry-baby."

I chose to accept Pete's opinion as fact until or unless it was proven otherwise. I only hoped that he was correct.

CHAPTER 28

I was calmer in the morning, and at the office bright and early, wanting to tie up as many loose ends as possible before heading off to parts unknown with Pete.

I called Jimmy Landry, my friend the arson investigator. I couldn't close the file on Andy's fire loss without knowing officially if the fire had been an accident or arson. We'd pay Andy either way, but if it was arson, New England Casualty and Indemnity could then attempt to recover from the guilty party. If we could identify him. Also, it was a good idea to keep in touch with Jimmy from time to time, to maintain friendly professional connections.

"It's nice to hear from you, Amy," he said. "What can I do for you today?"

"I'm hoping for a final determination on the Chadwick Street fire. Accident or arson? I'll need that information in order to put this claim to rest."

"Sorry. I wish I could help you there, but the evidence we have just doesn't scream one way or the other. Without further information, there's a better than even chance we may never know."

That was not what I wanted to hear, but I'd learn to live with it if I had to. "Thanks, Jimmy. Please keep me in the loop if anything turns up."

"You'll be the second to know. I'll be the first."

"Right," I said. "I'll be fine with second place."

The death of Andy's tenant Ellen James was weighing heavily on my mind. I couldn't dismiss the idea that it was related to all the other goings-on at Chadwick Street. And there was a way to find out. I rummaged in my purse for the name and number of the person who had called Andy. April Raymond. 617-950-8672. I punched in the number.

April was willing to speak with me about Ellen, but her agreement came with a variety of strings attached. I couldn't come to her house. She would meet me at the Dunkin' across from the Savin Hill T station. It had to be within the hour because she had to get to work after that. And she'd be wearing a disguise – oversized sunglasses and a red knit hat with earlaps. An attractive outfit, to be sure. Also, I was to buy her a jelly stick and a coffee with cream and two sugars. Sounded like a good plan to me. I always loved a little cloak and dagger. Not to mention jelly sticks.

I called an uber and headed to Savin Hill. A few minutes later, I was standing in line to fill April's order, and included a jelly stick for myself, my second in as many days. Why not? I deserved a treat now and then. I paid the bill, then spotted April at a small corner table with her back to the wall. I approached cautiously, concerned the girl might be as paranoid as she sounded on the phone.

"April? Hello. I'm Amy Lynch. Thanks for agreeing to see me." I placed her coffee and donut on the table and grabbed a business card from my pocket.

She studied the card for a moment then said, "Yeah. OK. Have a seat. I need to get this over with and get to work on time."

So much for small talk.

April craned her neck to look at every corner of the room, then sat back and removed her glasses. Her eyes were bloodshot and wide with terror. They darted all around the room. She kept the hat on, perhaps to maintain the disguise, maybe just to hide unsightly hat hair.

"Sorry about the disguise," she said. "But I've got to be careful. Don't want that creep to find me. Ever."

"Charlie Florescu?" I guessed.

"Who else? I freaked out when I heard the news last night. That he was out of jail and on the loose. He's one dangerous dude, you know. Scares the crap out of me."

He scared me as well, but April didn't need to know about my misadventure last night.

"Does he know where you live? Or where you work?" I asked her. "That could be a problem."

"Nope. And he never will. I'm making damn sure of that."

The look on her face belied the confidence of that statement. "Do you think Florescu would harm you?"

"Hell yes. In a heartbeat. He'd kill me, just like he killed Ellen."

Repressing my memories of the previous evening, I looked her straight in the blood-shot eyes. "Are you sure about that? He definitely killed Ellen?"

She let out a small sob.

I hated putting the poor girl through this inquisition, but felt there was no choice. "Please tell me what you know about Ellen James. And about how she died."

April took in a deep breath then let it out slowly. "Me and Ellen, we go way back. Went all through school together. Saint Gregory's in Dorchester. We were best friends, even after she took up with that damn Charlie. We didn't see each other too much after that. Charlie occupied most of her time. It was like he'd cast a spell on her or something. But she and I still talked a lot, pretty much any time Charlie wasn't around."

She sat back for a moment, as if to regroup.

I leaned in closer. "Go on."

"From what Ellen told me, Charlie treated her really bad. Knocked her around a lot. Fed her drugs. Bad stuff. Got her hooked. After a while she didn't even try to leave him. Just took his abuse. And his drugs. Lots of them. All of the time." She gulped her coffee.

I sampled my jelly stick. *Yum.* "What happened the day of the fire?"

"Charlie was out somewhere. When Ellen had to leave her apartment, she didn't know where to go. Early in the evening she showed up at my door. Said she'd been wandering around for hours not knowing what to do. And she was scared. Scared bad. Kept saying 'He's gonna kill me too.' I took her in, hoping to help her find a way to get clean and dump Charlie." She wiped a tear from her cheek. "Fool that I was. I should have known better. Just a waste of time."

"I'm so sorry. Ellen was lucky to have a friend like you. Are you sure it was Charlie she thought would kill her?"

"Had to be. Who else?"

One never knows who else, but I kept that thought to myself. "Please tell me what Ellen told you."

April took a large bite of her jelly stick and frowned while she chewed.

I waited as patiently as I could. Which wasn't very long.

Finally, April said, "Ellen told me she kicked Charlie out," April said. "After a big blow up. For once she had stood up to him. And he didn't like it. The cruel streak in him was getting out of control. It scared her. She said Charlie had been messing with one of those kids staying on the second floor. The ones who brought swords with them. Said they were all dorks. Charlie had offered to sell drugs to one of them. Set up a meeting with him in the cellar, of all the crazy places. Asked him to bring his sword and teach him how to use it. What Charlie really planned to do was jerk the guy around a bit, just for fun, then rob him. Ellen tried to talk him out of it. Charlie refused.

She told him to get out. He stomped out in a huff to meet up with that dork."

So that's how Howie Zupkoff ended up in the cellar. I knew Florescu had been involved somehow.

April took a big gulp of her coffee, then continued, "A few minutes later, Ellen looked out the window and saw Charlie running down the street like his pants were on fire. She was still all worked up after their fight. She went down to the cellar to smoke a joint to help her calm down. She couldn't smoke it in her apartment because the old lady on the first floor complained about the smell. Damn old grouch. She wasn't even around much lately, but Ellen wasn't looking for any trouble. Anyway, she got to the bottom of the stairs and lit up, then saw somebody. It was the new guy on the third floor. I don't remember his name."

"Douglas Weiss?"

"Right. He ran past her so fast he nearly knocked her over. Then she saw that other guy on the floor. The nerdy guy. The one Charlie was meeting. He was wearing a funny-looking white outfit, holding a sword and covered with blood. Ellen panicked. She dropped her joint and ran."

I finished the scenario for her. "And the joint landed on something flammable and started the fire."

"I guess so. Ellen said she was about half way up the stairs to her apartment when the smoke alarms started. She freaked, and ran outside without going back for a coat or even her purse. When she got to my place, she was freezing. All she had with her was her phone and a pocket full of pills. She was shaking, saying that Charlie had killed that guy and she'd be next."

That explained a lot. "Exactly how did Ellen die?"

"Charlie did it," April said. "I mean, it was his fault. He killed her with the pills he fed her. She went looking for him the next day. She had the shakes real bad. Decided she couldn't get clean. At least not right then. I went after her, hoping to change her mind. It didn't work. She told me to go away and leave her alone." April sobbed and blew her nose. "Next morning, I found Ellen's cell phone between the cushions on my couch. I went out looking for her to return it. Besides, I was real worried about what Charlie might do to her."

"And you found her?"

"Sure did. In an alley down the street from my place. Dead."

"How awful. What did you do?"

"I grabbed her phone and dialed 911. I didn't give them my name, though. Too scared they'd want me to be a witness against Charlie. I hated leaving Ellen there like that, but had no real choice. I was afraid I'd be next. I took off real quick before the cops got there."

As much as I didn't like the choice April had made, I could understand it. She was obviously terrified of Charlie Florescu. As was I.

"But you kept her phone," I said.

"Yeah. I don't really know why. It rang a lot, but I didn't answer it. I was worried it'd be Charlie and he'd come get me. That he'd use the phone to track me down. I finally checked the voicemails. Most of them were from Charlie. A few from that other guy. You know, the new landlord." She frowned. "And that's all I know."

"Thanks for telling me all this," I said. "Would it be all right with you if I repeated it to the police?"

"I guess so. Actually, you can give them Ellen's phone as well. I wish I could say I'd speak with them myself, but I'm just too damn scared."

I got that. Charlie Florescu scared me too.

April refused to give me her address. Still looking antsy, she put on her sunglasses. "Gotta go now or I'll be late for work."

And off she went before I could thank her for her help.

I needed to drop in on Detective Donnelly at once and fill him in on Ellen James.

I jumped on the T and took the train to Donnelly's office. The trip involved a short walk, but I was fine with that. The sun was out. And it gave me time to digest everything April Raymond had told me.

Luck was with me. Donnelly was in his office and willing to see me, albeit grudgingly. "What brings you here today?" he grunted, but didn't suggest I take a seat.

I sat anyway, and gave him the short version of my incident the night before.

Donnelly shook his head. "Son of a bitch. I'm glad you're all right. But are you really sure it was him? Not somebody else with a grudge against you?"

I silently resented that remark. "I have no proof, but my gut says it was him. What I can't figure out is how he knew who I was, or where to find me."

"Your name was listed as a witness on the complaint we filed against him the day we arrested him on Chadwick Street. I'm guessing that was all he needed to track you down."

"You may be right."

"Please tell me he's been found and is back in jail," I said.

"I wish I could. We're still looking for him. In the meantime, please be careful. Don't take any chances. Don't go out alone unless you have to."

I fought the impulse to say, "Thanks for the advice. I never would have thought of that." Better to stay on his good side. "I have some other information I believe you'll find interesting."

He grabbed a notebook and pen. "Shoot."

I gave him Ellen's phone, then repeated everything April Raymond had told me about both the origin of the fire and Ellen James' death.

"That agrees with what Mr. Yesley told us," he said. "It's a relief to put a name to that body in the alley. I'll let the medical examiner know." He frowned. "As much as I'd like to blame Charlie Florescu for that kid's death, let's not forget that Douglas Weiss was there as well. He could be involved. We need to pay him a visit. Something tells me you probably know his whereabouts."

"As far as I know, he's staying with Andy Yesley in Newton and helping with the repairs on Chadwick Street." I gave him the Newton address.

Donnelly sat back for a moment with his hands clasped at the back of his neck. "You interested in coming to work for us here?" he asked. "Something tells me you'd be good at it."

"No thanks."

"How come? We get pretty good benefits."

"You folks have to follow the rules. On my own, I have a lot more leeway." Might as well be up-front with the man.

"I'll pretend I didn't hear that. But thanks for the info."

"My pleasure," I said as I rose to leave. "Have a nice weekend."

Outside the police station, I called for an uber to return to my office, telephoning Jimmy Landry en route.

"Don't get me wrong, Amy. It's always nice to hear from you. But didn't I just speak with you a little while ago?"

"Yes," I told him. "And now I have the information we both need to close our respective cases." Once again, I repeated April Raymond's story.

Jimmy let out a long, slow whistle. "Son of a biscuit. Who would have thought it? Looks like my work here is done."

"And mine as well," I said. "At least as far as the fire was concerned. I am still trying to discover the story behind that poor little baby. I know it's outside my job description, but I just can't let it go. Besides, what I do with my own time over the weekend is my own business."

"If you learn something, please give me a call. Just to put my mind at ease."

"It's not an 'if', Jimmy. It's a 'when.'" I told him. And I was determined to make it so.

CHAPTER 29

Peggy jumped up from her desk when I arrived at the office. "Amy, hi. I'm so glad you're back."

It's always nice to be missed. "I'm guessing that means you have good news for me."

"News, yes. You can decide how good it is. And I wanted to tell you in person, but couldn't have waited much longer. I have to be out of here by 4:30."

"Big date tonight?" *Not to mention early.*

Peggy shook her head. "Nope. Big dentist appointment. And good old Dr. Kurtz gets cranky if I'm late."

"Don't they all? Still, they have no problem keeping their patients waiting. So tell me, what did you find?"

"Not what," she said. "More like who. Or should I say whom?"

"Please tell me it's Marissa Albert. That would make my week complete."

Peggy grinned from ear to ear as she pointed to her computer screen.

It was an obituary.

"Marissa is dead?" I asked. That would be a real bummer.

"Not that I know of," Peggy said.

"Then whose obituary is this?"

"Robert Albert, Jr."

I sat in her visitor's chair. "How about we take this from the top? When I left a while ago, you were going to do a Facebook and Google search for Marissa."

"Right. And it became a long and arduous task."

"That's why I asked you to do it. I hate arduous tasks. And, by the way, have you been reading the thesaurus again?"

She giggled. "What can I say? A girl needs a hobby. It's lucky for you I have a flair for these things. Not to mention patience. I went through dead end after dead end. Too many Marissa Alberts. I spent a lot of time in Facebook Hell reading about Marissa Albert the novelist. She turned out to be Asian. Then there were at least a dozen young professionals with the name, but none in the right age group. Same thing in the Registry of Motor Vehicles database. Nobody fit the profile. The White Pages listed twenty more women with the name, but none in the Berkshires. I had to resort to Google. You can't even begin to guess how many pages of absolute trivia I plowed through. And nobody sounded right. I was pretty much bug-eyed by the time I arrived here." She pointed to the death notice on her screen. "I found this little mention in the obituary section of the Berkshire Eagle."

"That sounds like a small local newspaper," I said.

"It is. In Lee, Massachusetts. That's where Robert Albert, Jr. lived and died. He was Marissa's father." Peggy scrolled down to a portion of the obituary which read: "Also survived by his daughter Marissa Albert of West Stockbridge."

"Son of a gun. Nice work, Peggy. It has to be her. Any mention of a grandchild in the obit?" I asked.

Peggy shook her head.

"I'm guessing they don't list a street address for the woman."

"Sorry."

"How old is the obituary?"

That brought a frown to Peggy's face. "Unfortunately nearly fourteen years. But West Stockbridge is a very small town. Even if Marissa's gone, there must be somebody there who'd remember her." She gave me her world-weary Friday afternoon look. "Do you want me to keep digging?"

"Actually, no. I think I'll take a drive out there over the weekend. Pete and I were planning a road trip anyway. We might as well go to the Berkshires."

"Really?" Peggy said, "I bet it'll be cold and snowy there."

"Pete and I are tough. We can handle a little winter weather."

"Do you want me to take care of Sam for you?" she asked.

"Thanks, but I think I'll bring him with us. He could use a weekend away too. And I know there's at least one pet-friendly inn in the area. Sam and I stayed there a couple of years ago." I smiled. "You just earned your salary for the week. Why don't you take the rest of the day off? And have a great weekend."

Peggy pointed to the clock on the wall. Nearly 4:30. "Thanks. See you Monday."

I finished up a few things at the office which couldn't wait until Monday, then called Pete. "Pack some warm clothes," I told him.

"If you say so. Does that mean you've decided where we're going this weekend?"

"It sure does. How do the Berkshires sound to you?"

"Cold and snowy, not to mention mountainous."

"Right on all counts, but that's where we're going. It'll be fine. And there are some fabulous restaurants in Lee, as well as a motel that welcomes pets, so Sam can come with us."

"I'm sure he'd like that. OK, then. The Berkshires it is."

I hesitated, then said, "I'll also need to do a bit of work while we're there, but there'll still be plenty of time for us." And I would do whatever I had to do to make that happen.

CHAPTER 30

I had always considered the Massachusetts Turnpike, aka Route 90, a boring road. Nothing but straight highway, complete with the requisite eighteen-wheelers spewing diesel exhaust and refusing to let you pass them. The back roads suited me better. They were more peaceful, more relaxing. They had nicer scenery. Sweeter smelling air. But this Saturday morning Pete and I were on a mission with no time for scenic tours. The roads less traveled would have to wait until another time.

The weather was fair and the traffic light. We were making good time, more than half-way there with only one pit stop. And that was more for Sam than for Pete or me. Sam was now snoozing happily on a blanket in the back seat of Pete's new Audi. The blanket was important. As much as he loved Sam, Pete also loved his leather upholstery. I had suggested taking my Mustang, but Pete wanted to put some miles on his new wheels, give it a good breaking in. And he always maintained his vehicles in pristine condition.

"Alone at last," Pete said as we headed west. "As fond as I am of my cousin Andy, I've been spending more time with him lately than with you. You and I need some good old-fashioned alone time.

It's been a while. What with your work, and my work and Andy's problems, we haven't had much down time together lately. I miss us."

I seconded that emotion. "You're right about that. And we'll make up for it this weekend. Big time." I put my phone in my lap. "We're all set for a room. The Stockbridge Country Inn is happy to accommodate Sam as well as us. They have a first floor room available with a door opening onto a dog park out back. Sounds perfect."

Pete smiled. "That's great. I know this is a working weekend for you, but a bit of country charm never hurts. It's good to get out of the rat-race."

That was my cue. "I spoke with my parents the other day. My dad told me an old law school friend of his is planning to move to Florida."

Pete nodded, apparently more interested in the road ahead than in my father's old friends.

"This guy is an attorney. He's looking to sell both his law practice and his home, then retire to Florida. I wondered if you might be interested."

That got Pete's attention. "Interested in retiring to Florida?"

"At some point, sure. But in the meantime, what do you think about maybe buying this fellow's law practice?"

"Any particular type of law?"

"Nope. According to my dad, it's general practice. In a small town."

He turned in my direction. "Where?"

"Walpole. And keep your eyes on the road, please."

Pete broke into a broad grin. "Really? Walpole's right near Massapoag Junction, isn't it?"

"Yes, it is."

"What do you know about this guy?"

"His name is Will Granger. I've known him and his wife Gracie all my life. They're nice. Will and my dad went to Suffolk Law

School together decades ago. Professionally speaking, I don't know much about the man."

"But if he's a friend of your dad's, he's probably a stand-up guy."

"You could Google him to see what else you can learn. Do you want me to ask my dad to introduce you to him?"

"It can't hurt to talk to him. And Lord knows I'm ready for a change. I can't take much more of the corporate bullshit at my office."

"I'll let Dad know." That settled for the time being, I closed my eyes to think through what I needed to do in Stockbridge, what I hoped to learn.

Pete beat me to the punch. "What do you know about this woman we're looking for?"

"Marissa Albert. I don't know much of anything. Only her name and a general location. And the fact that she moved back here around twenty years ago. She's probably somewhere in her mid-forties."

"How do you plan to find her with only those few facts?"

"I thought I'd start at the public library. Which shouldn't be too far from here."

"Why the library?" He gave me an odd look. "Do you think she works there?"

"My poor prosaic Pete, and I say that with an abundance of love. Use your imagination. I know you've got one somewhere deep down inside you. The library should have old telephone books somewhere, at least on microfiche. We'll start with that. Those books can be a fountain of information." I pointed to the West Stockbridge exit.

Pete put on his blinker and moved into the right lane. "A town as small as West Stockbridge has a public library?"

I laughed. "Sure does. Just under two thousand citizens and most of them probably know how to read. The library's on Main Street."

"Do you think they'll be open on a Saturday?"

I held up my phone to show him the website. "It says here they're open today from 10:00 to 4:00."

West Stockbridge was a pretty little country town, with all the charm one would expect in the Berkshires, complete with snow so newly-fallen it hadn't yet had time to get dirty. Or maybe out here it stayed clean and white. One could hope. The downtown area was larger than I expected and busy on a Saturday morning.

Pete located the library and parked the car. "How about Sam and I take a stroll down Main Street while you do your thing in there?"

Sam perked up at the sound of his name, always eager to explore someplace new.

"Good plan," I said. "I'll meet you back here in half an hour."

We went our separate ways.

I came out of the library twenty minutes later to find Pete and Sam playing Frisbee in the snow in front of the library. Sam grabbed the Frisbee and brought it to me.

"We'll play later, Buddy," I told him. "Right now I have work to do."

Pete joined us. "That was pretty clever of you thinking to use an old telephone book. Where'd you learn a trick like that?"

"From Kinsey Millhone."

"Is that a friend of yours? Somebody I should know?"

I shook my head. Apparently Pete had never read Sue Grafton.

Pete cocked his head in an "oh-well" sort of way. "What did you learn?"

I held up a piece of paper. "Name, address and phone number for Marissa Albert, all twenty years old."

"A good start. Did you try the number?"

"Sure did," I said. "No longer in service."

"Then what's next?" Pete asked. "I'm sure you have a plan in mind."

Of course I did. "Let's drive to the address and knock on the door. And if that doesn't work, we'll speak with the neighbors.

Somebody is sure to know something." I punched the address into the GPS on my phone. "OK. Let's boogie."

The house at 37 Glendale Road was old and in need of paint. What little shrubbery there was looked like topiary gone bad. The snow on the front walk was newly-shoveled. An old blue Toyota sat in the driveway. Somebody lived there.

Pete waited in the car with Sam while I approached the house and rang the bell.

"Hang on," a large voice bellowed from beyond the door. "Be there in a minute."

And it was a full minute before the door opened. I couldn't imagine what had taken the man so long. The house wasn't all that big.

A beer-bellied middle-aged man in a sleeveless undershirt stood before me. He looked like the kind of guy who might give a girl lug nuts for her birthday. Definitely not my type.

"Whatever you're selling, we don't want it," he growled.

I forced the sweetest smile I could muster. "I'm not selling anything. I'm looking for a woman who used to live at this address. Her name was Marissa Albert."

"Never heard of her," he said. "And I've lived her nearly ten years. Bought the place from a fellow named Evers. Or something like that. Sorry I can't help you." And he closed the door in my face.

Not to be discouraged, I knocked on the next-door neighbor's door. No answer. Same at the next house. I crossed the street, hoping to do better there. I glanced into the car on the way. Sam was resting; Pete was on his phone.

I rang the bell on the house directly across from number 37.

A grandmotherly woman in a checkered apron answered. "Hello, Dear. Can I do something for you?"

"I hope so." I smiled. "I'm looking for a woman named Marissa Albert. She used to live across the street here."

"Marissa. Of course I remember her. Such a nice girl. She moved away about a dozen years ago."

Sometimes things just work out right. "Do you know where she went?"

The woman paused in thought. "Maybe. She got married. To a fellow named Arnold. That's his last name. I can't remember the first."

"That's all right. The last name is a big help. Do you know where they moved to?"

"Great Barrington," she told me. "Though like I said, that was a dozen years ago. They could be living anywhere by now."

I thanked the woman profusely, wished her a lovely day and returned to the car.

Pete and Sam both gave me expectant looks. "Any luck?" Pete asked.

"A place to start," I said as I punched some info into my phone.

"And that place would be ...?"

"Great Barrington."

"What's in Great Barrington?"

"With any luck, Marissa Albert Arnold."

CHAPTER 31

Pete put the car in gear. I filled him in on what I had learned as I punched the Arnolds' address into the GPS.

"Do you want to call ahead?" he asked. "To make sure she'll be home."

"Hell, no. I don't want to give her a heads-up and spook her. If she has time to think about it, she may refuse to see me. This is going to be a tough enough conversation as it is. I need to find a way to ease into it. Or bushwhack the woman." I had to figure out how I was going to do that. Fast.

We arrived at 110 State Road in Great Barrington twenty minutes later. It was a modest house in a modest neighborhood. Neat, well-kept, with a shiny new blue SUV in the driveway.

Pete and Sam stayed in the car. I held my breath as I rang the doorbell.

The door opened half-way to reveal a woman in her forties with light brown hair and blue eyes. She might have been pretty if only she'd smile.

"Yes?" she said, keeping the door half closed.

"Are you Mrs. Arnold?" I asked, crossing my fingers.

"I am," she said, a note of hesitance in her voice. "Can I do something for you?"

The look on her face suggested she wasn't a bit interested in doing anything for me. Nevertheless, I forged on. "My name is Amy Lynch. I'm a friend of Ursula Fagan's, from Chadwick Street."

She gasped. Her eyes grew wide and her jaw dropped. "Chadwick Street? Dear God! That was a lifetime ago. I try not to think about those days." A dark cloud settled over her face. "Did Richard send you to find me?" she asked me. "Is that why you're here?"

"No, he didn't."

"Do you know where he is?"

"I think so, but I also know you don't need to be afraid of him anymore," I told her, hoping my reassurance didn't sound as lame as I thought it did.

"Then how did you find me?"

"With a little help from Ursula Fagan. And a lot of time online." I spoke softly, calmly, trying to keep her from panicking. "I'm hoping to speak with you about the time when you lived on Chadwick Street."

A voice bellowed from inside the house. "Who is it, Marissa? What do they want?"

"It's all right, Chet," Marissa called back. "I've got this. It's nothing important." She turned to me and spoke in a near whisper. "How did you know my new name? What do you want from me?" Her voice quivered as she spoke.

"How I found you is not important, though Ursula certainly helped. And I don't want anything from you. But I do have some information I think you'll want to hear."

Her eyes narrowed as she studied me. "All right. I'll listen to you. But not now. My husband and kids are home. We need to do this in private."

Oh dear! Had she not told her husband about her life in Dorchester? That could make things really sticky, really fast. I felt

174

like an intruder. I came here thinking I was doing something good for this woman, not disrupting her life.

"OK," she said. "Tell you what. Chet and the kids have a Boy Scout event this afternoon. Come back around 3:00 and I'll listen to what you have to say."

Whew! That was a relief. "Sounds good," I said. "See you then."

She closed the door before I could say anything further.

Back in the car, I gave Pete an update.

He looked at his watch. "It's nearly 11:30. Shall we go back to Stockbridge and check in to the Inn? Maybe relax a bit." He gave me an amorous leer.

I shook my head. "Sorry. I wish we could. And we definitely will relax later. But the room won't be ready until 2:00. Let's grab an early lunch somewhere. And Sam will be needing a walk soon."

"It's too bad Alice's Restaurant is gone," Pete said. "It would've been fun to eat there."

He was silent for a moment, a pensive look on his face. "If we head back to Stockbridge, we could visit the Norman Rockwell Museum. I've heard it's worth the trip."

I'd never known Pete to be an art lover. My guy was full of surprises. And so far, they were all good.

"I see a park up the street," he said. "How about we pull in and let Sam take care of business and get a breath of fresh air before we head out?"

Sam's business taken care of, we found a little place for lunch on Main Street in Stockbridge. Quaint without being annoyingly cutesy. Homemade beef stew, accompanied by freshly-baked bread still warm from the oven. Not bad. We also ordered a cup of stew to go for Sam. My buddy deserved a treat for waiting so patiently in the car.

As tasty as the stew was, I couldn't give it my full attention. I was too antsy about Marissa Albert, now Arnold. "I hope I'm doing the right thing," I said to Pete. "Marissa has a new life here, a new husband, a family. Maybe I shouldn't be dredging up bad memories for her."

Pete gave me an adorable smile. "Not to worry, Ames. You're doing right. The woman deserves to know her baby has been found. She deserves to give him a decent burial. Closure is important, you know."

I supposed he was right. But I still couldn't relax. Before I had finished my stew, my phone rang. Boston Police. Yikes! "Sorry, Pete," I said. "I have to take this. It could be important." I stepped out to the sidewalk.

"Hello?"

"Ms. Lynch, hi. Frank Donnelly here."

"Working on a Saturday, Detective? That's very dedicated of you."

"What can I say? I have no life," he laughed. "And what about you? You must be working too or you wouldn't have answered my call."

"Guilty as charged," I laughed. "However, I am also in the Berkshires for the weekend. And my boyfriend is with me."

"Lucky you. What work brings you to the Berkshires? Anything I should know about?"

"I'll tell you all about it when I get back," I said, hoping I'd actually have some news for him by then.

"You sure you don't want to tell me now?"

"Can't do that. I'm not sure yet how things will turn out." Perhaps a bit of mystery would brighten the detective's day.

"Whatever," he said. "Anyway, the reason for my call is this. We've got Charlie Florescu in custody. Nabbed him last night. I thought you'd want to know."

He was correct. Not to mention thoughtful. "How did you find him?"

"Got a hot tip. From that nosy lady next door on Chadwick Street."

"Mrs. Czwakiel?"

"Yeah. Right. She called at 2:00 A.M. to say someone was trying to break into number twelve again."

Insomnia can be a wonderful thing.

"The good news is we got the guy," Donnelly continued. "Now we can add attempted breaking and entering to the charges against him. Not to mention probably animal cruelty."

"You heard about Fifi then?"

"Sure did. Mrs. Czwakiel is as thorough as she is nosy. And we love her for it. Hell of a name for a dog, though."

I couldn't argue with that.

"Florescu should be going away for a long time now." Donnelly hesitated, then added, "And if we need a witness against him, might you be available?"

"Not a problem, Detective. It would be my pleasure."

"Great. Thanks."

"What about Weiss?" I asked. "Any news on him?"

"Nope. No sign of him on Chadwick Street or at the Newton address. The guy's in the wind. But not to worry. We'll catch up with him eventually. We always do."

I wasn't worried. "At some point, he'll probably show up in the last place you'd expect to find him."

"If you say so," Donnelly said. "Anyway, that's all for now. I just wanted to keep you up-to-date."

"And I appreciate it," I told him. "Enjoy the rest of your weekend."

"You too. And by the way, give that boyfriend of yours a message for me."

"And what would that be?"

"Tell him he's a lucky guy."

I hoped Pete already knew that, but it was nice to hear.

My stew was cold when I returned inside. I ate it anyway. And washed it down with lukewarm tea. I'd need the sustenance to get through my conversation with Marissa. Then Pete and I brought Sam his stew and headed off to the Rockwell Museum.

The museum was nice. Pete really got into the whole Americana thing. I liked it as well, but found myself sneaking peeks at my watch every few minutes. I wanted to be right on time arriving at Marissa's house. Maybe even a few minutes early. I didn't want to give her the chance to change her mind and run.

CHAPTER 32

Pete and I pulled up in front of Marissa's house in time to see her coming out the front door. Skipping out on us? Sure looked that way.

I approached her on the front walk. "Hello, Marissa, you're not leaving, are you? Please don't. You really need to hear what I have to say."

She gave me a deer-in-the-headlight look. "You caught me. I panicked and was about to chicken out. Sorry."

"There's nothing to be sorry about," I said, "as long as you'll speak with me now."

Marissa slumped. "Oh well, I guess you might as well come in." She pointed to Pete's car. "What about him? Who is he?"

"My boyfriend Pete. My dog Sam is with him. They'll be fine in the car."

Marissa gave me a disinterested look as I followed her into the house. "OK," she said. "We've got about an hour and a half until Chet and the kids get home." She let out a weary sigh. "I guess I always knew it would all catch up with me one day. No matter how hard you try, you can't run away forever. OK. Let's hear what you have to tell me." She sank into a chair.

179

I made myself as comfortable as I could under the circumstances and began my story. "There was a fire at the house on Chadwick Street."

"A fire? Please tell me that Richard Grant perished in it, or at least lost everything he owned. Or maybe that he started it, then got arrested and is going to jail for life."

Still bitter after all these years. From what Ursula Fagan had told me about Grant, I couldn't blame Marissa. "I work as an investigator for the company that insures the property. That's how I met Ursula. I went to interview her about the fire."

"Goodness, I haven't thought about Ursula in years. She and I were quite friendly a very long time ago. One of my few real friends in Boston. How is she?"

"She's doing well enough," I said. "The Multiple Sclerosis is getting the better of her these days. She doesn't get out much anymore."

"I'm sorry to hear that. I didn't know about the MS."

"Ursula is living with her daughter in Quincy. I went there to speak with her. And she told me about you and Richard."

Marissa frowned. "It's not a very pretty story, is it? I still don't understand how you found me. Or why."

"Ursula knew your maiden name. It was on your wedding invitation. Believe it or not, she saved it all these years. She also kept the letter you sent her after you left, so she knew you were somewhere in this area. With that much information, it was easy enough to track you down online."

"I'll take your word for it."

Now came the tough part. I steeled myself and said, "The fire started in the cellar of Chadwick Street."

"I always hated that place. It was dark and creepy. And it smelled like mold. I only went down there when I had no choice."

"The arson investigator and the police were down there, trying to determine the cause of the fire." I held my breath for a moment hoping to find the right words. "They found an old suitcase buried there. It contained the remains of a baby."

Marissa blanched. "Dear God. My Timmy. Richard must have buried him there after I ran." Her hands shook as she wiped tears from her cheeks.

"That's right. Richard's fingerprints were all over the suitcase." I handed her a packet of tissues from my purse, grateful that I had come prepared, then sat back and waited for her to collect herself.

After a few unsteady moments, Marissa said, "I've never spoken with anybody about what happened. I've spent years trying to put it all behind me. To pretend it never happened. Besides, I was afraid."

"Of what?" I asked. "Or whom?"

"Of Richard. It was like he was two different people. When I first met him he was charming, fun, everything I thought I wanted in a husband. It wasn't until after we were married that I saw his dark side. And it was very, very dark. He'd be sweet and loving one minute, then the next he'd go into a violent rage for no apparent reason. I realize now that he must have had some sort of bi-polar disorder."

It sure sounded that way to me.

"But it wasn't just fear of Richard," Marissa continued. "I was also worried about the trouble I could be in if anybody knew."

I gave her a moment to compose herself, then asked, "Knew what?"

Marissa ignored the tears running down her cheeks. "Richard killed Timmy. Maybe not on purpose, but he still killed him. He shook my baby to death because the poor little guy wouldn't stop crying. Richard was in a terrifying rage. I thought he'd kill me next. Timmy was beyond help at that point. I ran away in a panic, to save my own life. I only got out alive because Richard was too drunk to stop me. I should have gone straight to the police. I know that now. Back then I wasn't thinking straight. I was too scared for my own safety."

Marissa was right. She should have told the police. But I understood why she hadn't. We'd deal with that later. Detective Donnelly would find a way to make it all right. "So what did you do?" I asked.

"I made it to a friend's house. She gave me some money, helped me to get back here, to my father's house. My mother was gone by then. Dad greeted me with a nasty 'I told you so.' Dad never did like Richard. Living with my father wasn't easy, but at least I was safe. I never told him anything about Timmy. I simply couldn't deal with the guilt. And that awful night has haunted me ever since."

"Of course it has," I said. "It must have been terrible for you. So sad, and so frightening."

She stared at the floor. "I was afraid for a long time. Worried that Richard would find me somehow. I was scared and sad and depressed. I thought about killing myself more than once. Then I met Chet, and began to wonder if maybe life could be all right again."

She grabbed another tissue and blew her nose. "The only person I ever told about Timmy was Father Williams at St. Joseph's in Stockbridge. I told him in confession, so couldn't repeat anything. He listened to my story. He didn't judge me. Eventually he helped me get my marriage to Richard annulled so Chet and I could be married in the church. My life has been good since then. Quiet. Peaceful. I have a nice husband. He's a local cop. Good kids. A part-time job at the bookstore downtown. I have no complaints. I'm safe here. And happy."

"And here I am bringing back all those awful memories," I said. "I am truly sorry to do that. But I thought you deserved to know we'd found your baby's remains."

Marissa gave me a small, sad smile. "You mean so I can lay him to rest at last."

"Correct. I hope I made the right decision."

"You did," she said. "As much as it hurts, I needed to know. Now maybe I can find a way to work through the guilt. And be free of the nightmares."

We sat in silence for a few moments and let the reality of the situation sink in.

Marissa stared off into the distance. Finally, she said, "What do I do now?"

"That's up to you. Would you come to Boston to meet with the police and the coroner? So they can release Timmy's remains to you?"

"I don't know if I can do that," she said.

That wasn't the answer I wanted, but I could understand how she felt.

"The problem is that my husband doesn't know all this," she said. "He knows about Richard, but nothing about my baby. I was afraid that if he knew he'd make me report it to the police. Like I told you, he's a cop. So I lived a lie all these years."

"Can you bring yourself to tell him the whole truth now?"

"I think I have to. I don't know how I'm going to do it, but he has to know. Chet loves me. I know that. He'll understand. He'll find a way to help me."

I hoped she was right about that.

"Let me speak with him this evening," Marissa said, "once the kids are in bed. I'll tell him the whole sad story. Can I call you tomorrow and let you know what I've decided to do?"

"Absolutely." I gave her my card with my cell number on the back. "But please don't take too long. At some point, the coroner will have to make a decision concerning your baby. And I don't want you having any regrets."

"You mean any more regrets," she said. "I'll call you tomorrow one way or the other."

I knew what I hoped she'd decide. And said a prayer that she would do so.

CHAPTER 33

After we checked into the Inn, Pete bundled up in a warm hat, a scarf and gloves, then he and Sam went to the dog park. Sam had been a wonderful sport so far and not complained at all about being stuck in the car most of the day. I didn't want to push my luck, though. He and Pete could both use some fresh air and exercise.

While the guys were out, I did a bit of research online and found a French bistro called Chez Nous just a few miles away in Lee. The menu was to my liking and the place got great reviews. I made a 6:00 reservation.

"Why so early?" Pete asked when I told him.

"It's Saturday night. The place was almost fully booked. It was either 6:00 or 9:00. I was pretty sure I couldn't wait until 9:00. Besides, an early dinner will give us more time afterward. I'm sure we'll come up with some way to spend it." I gave him my best phony leer.

He gave me a gorgeous smile in return, dimples and all. "Good plan."

Thirty minutes later, we were showered, changed and out the door.

"Hold on," Pete said as we approached his car. "You forgot your cell phone. I saw it on the bed."

"I didn't forget anything," I told him. "This evening is about us. No distractions or interruptions. Just a lovely meal and some 'us' time."

Chez Nous was small and charming. And packed even at 6:00. It was a good thing I had called when I did. We ordered cocktails. Since I wasn't driving, I decided on scotch. Pete ordered the same, even though he was driving. He could hold his liquor better than I could.

We studied the menu.

"What looks good to you?" Pete asked.

"Boeuf bourguignon. One of my favorite French dishes. And I can get an additional half portion of it for Sam. What about you?"

"I'm trying to decide between scallops and cod. It's a tough decision."

"It shouldn't be. Seafood isn't local out here. You might do better with meat, particularly on a cold January evening." I bit my tongue as I realized how bossy that sounded. I hoped Pete knew I was only trying to be helpful.

Luckily, he didn't appear to be offended. "Good point. I'll try the rack of lamb instead, although that's not really local either. It's from New Zealand." He winked at me.

Sometimes I just can't win. "And if we're both having red meat, we can share a bottle of red wine," I said. We settled on a Chateauneuf-du-Pape. It was expensive, but what the Hell? Good French wine is always worth the price.

I reached out and took Pete's hand. "This is nice. Thank you for being patient today and not complaining about all the time you spent sitting in the car. I'm sure that wasn't what you had envisioned for our weekend getaway. It was supposed to be about helping you unwind and forget your troubles."

"And I've been doing exactly that. I started a novel and actually got through several chapters so far. Believe it or not, it's the first time in ages I've read something other than a legal brief or a judge's decision. It was a rare treat."

"My poor Pete. That's so sad. It's also conclusive evidence that it's time to leave your job and move on to something that allows you to have an actual life."

"I'll drink to that." He toasted me with his water glass.

The waiter arrived at that moment with our cocktails. "Have you decided on your meals?" he asked.

"Not yet," I lied. "We want to relax and enjoy our drinks for a while."

The waiter nodded and left us alone.

"There was one other thing I did while you were busy interviewing people," Pete said.

"What was that?"

"I gave some serious thought to your father's friend who's looking to sell his law practice. It may just be the solution to my current quandary. I'd definitely like to learn more about it."

"I'll speak with my dad and get you the details."

"Too bad it's all contingent on the guy also selling his house. January is not the best time of year for the real estate market."

I grinned. "Not to worry. We'll stop by the fellow's home some day when nobody's around and bury St. Joseph in his yard."

Pete's eyes grew wide. "I have no idea how to respond to that. For one thing, we'd be trespassing. And I thought St. Joseph died a very long time ago."

"Not the real St. Joseph." I laughed. "Just a statue of him. You bury it face down in the yard and he helps you to sell your house."

Pete rolled his eyes. "Whoever told you such a thing?"

"My mother."

"I guess that means it must be true."

"Mom wouldn't lie to me. And it worked for my sister when she moved to Baltimore."

"If you say so." He shrugged. "At least, when I find a house in the suburbs I won't have to worry about selling my condo in Boston. Renting was a good idea. And I'm pretty sure a mortgage payment on a small house in a town like Massapoag Junction would be less money than the crazy high rents in Boston."

We ordered our meals, then spent the next hour dining like true gourmets and chatting about nothing of consequence. We needed to do this more often.

We declined the waiter's offer of after-dinner drinks. They tended to make me sleepy and I didn't want that. Pete and I still had the whole evening together. The last thing I wanted to do was fall asleep.

Back in our room, I treated Sam to his portion of boeuf bourguignon. He scarfed it down in no time, then gave us his "I'd like to go to the restroom now" look. Pete volunteered to take him.

While they were out attending to business, I noticed there was a voicemail on my cell phone. Mrs. Czwakiel. "Please call me back as soon as you can," she said. "Bad things are happening on Chadwick Street."

I held my breath as I hit the call-back button. What could have happened now? I was almost afraid to find out.

"Amy," Mrs. Czwakiel said. "Thank God it's you. I've been so upset I didn't know what to do. I still don't."

The woman sounded on the verge of tears, or perhaps a breakdown. Either way, it didn't bode well.

"Please, calm yourself, then tell me what's happening."

"Pretty much everything. And it's all bad. First it was Fifi, you know, the boys' dog. From across the street. Fifi's injuries were bad. She had to be put down. The boys are devastated, inconsolable. That dog was their child."

"I am really sorry," I told her. "I feel the same way about my dog Sam."

"I knew you'd understand." She paused, as if collecting her thoughts. "And it gets worse."

Oh dear. This was not good news. "Tell me, please."

"Beatrice was mugged today. In broad daylight, when she was walking home from visiting with me."

"How awful! Is she …?" I couldn't get the words out.

"She's alive, but in bad condition. Really bad. I'm worried she might not make it."

"Did she see who did it? Could she identify him?"

"Sadly, no. She was jumped from behind. Who would want to do such a thing to a sweet old lady? And why?"

"I wish I knew," I told her. "I wish I knew. Listen, I'm out in the Berkshires right now, but will be home late tomorrow. I'll see you sometime Monday. Please promise me you'll be very careful until the police catch the person who mugged Beatrice."

"Absolutely. I'm not planning on leaving my house any time soon." She paused, took a noisy breath, then added, "Actually, I'm afraid there's something else as well."

Good Lord. What else could there be? "Tell me, please."

"It's about the house next door."

Not again! What could be happening there now? "What about it?"

"Last night I heard a noise. Like glass breaking. I turned on my outside light and saw that a window into the cellar was broken. One of the brand new windows that Andy had just put in."

"Did you call the police?"

"Yes. And they got the guy. It was Charlie Florescu. I'm happy to say they took him away in handcuffs."

"That's great," I said. And it agreed with what Detective Donnelly had told me.

"Then I called Andy," she continued. "I knew he'd want to know. And he came right away to board it up."

"In the dark?"

"Yes. He was worried about animals getting in. We do have a few raccoons in the neighborhood."

Raccoons in the city? Who knew?

"I just don't know what's happening around here. This used to be such a nice neighborhood. Everybody knew everybody else. I always felt safe here. But not anymore. Bad things are happening. Bad people are doing them. It worries me."

I was worried as well. "Promise me you'll be careful."

"Always."

Mrs. Czwakiel was right. Bad things were indeed happening. But I had an idea it would all be over soon.

CHAPTER 34

Sunday morning dawned gray and damp, the precipitation more sleet than snow. Pete and I took one look at the nasty weather and went right back to sleep, a rare treat for both of us.

The ringing of my cell phone woke us about an hour later. Marissa Arnold.

"Good morning, Marissa," I said. "How are you?"

"I'm O.K." She paused.

I waited.

Finally she said, "Listen, I did like I said I would. I talked to my husband Chet last night. Told him the whole ugly story. Richard, Timmy, all of it."

"That must have been very difficult for you," I said. "Reliving such sad moments from the past."

"You have no idea," she said.

She was right about that. "And ...?"

"Chet and I decided to go to Boston. To make things right. We need to bury my baby. My Timmy needs to rest in peace." She let out a sob. "And to meet with the police if that's what has to happen."

"Thank you, Marissa. You won't regret your decision."

190

"I hope you're right," she said. "I've got a life here. A good life. I don't want to lose it. But it's time to put the old life to rest now. I know I can do it. As long as Chet is by my side, I'm sure I can."

Whew! "When can you come?"

"How about tomorrow? I'm off all day. And Chet is working the night shift, so he's free during the day."

"Tomorrow is great. Shall I meet you at the police station?"

"I can't believe I'm saying this," she said, "but I'd like to meet at the house on Chadwick Street. It'll be hard to see the place again, but I need to go there. I need to face my demons and put them to rest. I need to see where my Timmy has lain all these years. I mean, if that's all right with you."

"Of course it is," I told her. It was exactly what I wanted to happen.

"If we leave here good and early, we can probably arrive by around ten. How's that?"

"That's excellent," I said. "I'll see you then." I'd call Detective Donnelly and the medical examiner on the drive home. I knew I was taking a chance that they might not be available to speak with Marissa, but I also knew they were both eager to see the end of this case. My guess was that they'd make themselves available.

Pete returned from taking Sam outside. "It is one nasty day out there."

"That's a shame," I told him. "I was really hoping we could visit the Shaker Village in Hancock before heading home. I was there once years ago. It's a pretty interesting place."

He gave me a curious look. "I don't know much of anything about the Shakers, except that I think they're pretty much gone now. What's so interesting about them?"

"For one thing, they invented clothes pins."

"Useful, but not all that fascinating. Anything else?"

"They believed in total celibacy."

"Which explains their demise," Pete said. "Anyway, we can do that another time. The weather forecast says this storm is pretty much confined to the Berkshires. How about we take the scenic route back to Boston?"

"And where might this scenic route take us?" I had an idea what he had in mind.

"Massapoag Junction. I'd like you to see it. Maybe we can get a late lunch there."

I was right. "Sure," I told him. "Why not?"

We packed our things and headed out.

Once we were out of the Berkshires and the messy weather, I placed a call to Ted Rosen the medical examiner. I got his voicemail. No surprise there. Lots of people don't spend Sunday mornings at the office. I left a message explaining about Marissa and asking if he could find some time on Monday to meet with her and handle whatever arrangements were necessary concerning the baby's remains.

My next call was to Detective Donnelly. He answered on the first ring.

"I knew it. You are a witch!" he said. "I was just about to give you a call."

"And I expected simply to leave you a message. Not to find you at work on a Sunday morning. You weren't kidding the other day. You really do have no life."

"What can I tell you?" he said. "Chalk it up to dedication to duty. Anyway, how the hell did you know?"

"Know what?"

"That the prints would match. The coffee cup you gave me. We got a hit. The prints were in the system from Grant's manslaughter conviction. And they match the prints on the suitcase the baby's body was in. Douglas Weiss is Richard Grant."

Aha! I was right. "That's good news, Detective. Thank you for letting me know."

"Something tells me you already knew. How'd you figure it out?" he asked.

"A lucky guess," I said. No point in sharing all my tricks with him.

I filled him in on my conversations with Marissa.

"Well, haven't you just been a busy lady? And you talk about me working on the weekend."

"Touché," I said. "Can you meet us tomorrow on Chadwick Street? Maybe around ten thirty?" That would give Marissa some time at the property before dealing with the police. I suspected she'd need it.

"Absolutely," he told me. "Might be closer to 11:00 by the time I get there though."

"That's great. And who knows, maybe Richard Grant will show up as well."

"Wouldn't that be nice? We can always hope. OK, I'll see you then. And, by the way, nice work."

I ended the call and turned to Pete. "Just one more call. Then you can have my full and undivided attention."

"Not a problem," he said. "This is the boring part of the ride. Listening to you is keeping me entertained. I try to guess the other side of the conversation."

"Whatever works." I smiled at him, then dialed Andy.

"Good morning, Amy."

"Is everything all right, Andy? You sound rushed."

"Actually, I am. Getting ready for my best friend's wedding. I'm in a rush. I was out late last night, at the rehearsal dinner. I overslept this morning. And I have to be there on time. I'm the best man."

"I promise I'll only keep you a minute."

"O.K. You're on the clock."

"I heard you were on Chadwick Street last night."

"Had to. Because of the wedding today. I wanted to be sure no night critters got into the cellar."

"Right. Did you go into the cellar?"

"Nope. It was too late. And too dark. I just boarded it up from outside."

"Did you see anything inside? Or anybody?"

"Nary a thing, nor a soul. Why? Should I have?"

I ignored his question and moved on. "How am I doing time-wise?"

"You're OK so far."

"Good. Last question. How well secured are the doors into the cellar?"

"I did what you said. The broken bulkhead is boarded up from inside. The interior door to the cellar is boarded up as well, nailed shut and secured with a padlock. I've got the only key. Nobody is getting in there. Nobody but me."

"What about the back door?"

"Locked. You and I have keys. So do the police."

"Nice work. Will you be there tomorrow?"

"Sure will."

"I'll see you then."

"Anything in particular on your agenda?"

"Just a few loose ends. Enjoy the wedding."

"That was interesting," Pete said. "I had forgotten about the wedding. Is that why you didn't tell him about Marissa, and the baby, and the coroner and the ME? And everything else that's going on?"

"Sort of. That way he can enjoy today and deal with the rest tomorrow morning." Or something like that.

Pete exited the Mass. Turnpike and reverted to a series of back roads. Scenic, quiet, relaxing. And the sun came out! We drove through Walpole to check out the house my father's lawyer friend had on the market. Not a bad place, but Pete wasn't interested in it. It seemed he had his heart set on Massapoag Junction, just a few miles away.

DIRECT ELIMINATION

Our drive-through tour of the village was nice. Pete was right. It was a charming little spot. We had a late lunch at a cozy little restaurant on Main Street, a large enough meal that we wouldn't need any dinner. Then I was eager to get home and have a good night's sleep. I had a feeling Monday was going to be an interesting day.

CHAPTER 35

I arrived at the house on Chadwick Street early Monday morning, eager to see how the day would play out. And more than a little apprehensive.

The ServPro truck was parked out front. I wondered how much longer the job would take them. Andy was there as well, wearing a well-stocked tool belt over a gray corduroy jacket. His knit gloves had the fingers cut out. Good look.

"Love the new belt," I told him.

He shrugged. "It makes the job a little easier. Lord knows there's a lot of work to do around here. And I'm working alone at the moment."

Interesting development. "What happened to your helper Douglas Weiss?"

"Beats me. The last time I saw him was early Saturday morning. He said he had a few things to do and took off. Not long after that, the police came by my place wanting to talk to him. Any idea what that's all about?"

"I really couldn't say. Maybe he'll show up today." At least I hoped he would, but I didn't mention that to Andy. "What's your plan for the day?"

He frowned. "First of all, letting the ServPro crew into the cellar. The police called to tell me it was all right. After that, it's nothing but a few repairs and some paint. I got here over an hour ago. Wanted to double-check the dimensions of that busted window before buying a new one. I parked on Dover Street and walked around the rear of the house only to find the back door had been vandalized as well." He pointed to a gaping hole where a door had obviously been removed. "It was beyond repair. I pulled it off and ordered a new one right away. It'll be delivered in about an hour, along with the new cellar window and the new front door. This is getting expensive."

"Don't worry about that," I told him. "NEC&I will pay for most of it. I just can't believe you've had additional vandalism, though. It really stinks."

"Sure does. Whatever Charlie Florescu was looking for here, he must want it real bad." He shook his head. "Thank goodness the guy is behind bars now."

"He was probably trying to retrieve the drugs and cash Detective Donnelly removed from the freezer," I said.

"Then why did he want to get into the cellar?" Andy asked. "Do you think he had stuff stashed down there as well?"

"Could be. But what I don't understand is why he felt the need to destroy the rear door when the front door was nothing but plywood. Wouldn't it have been easier to break in there?"

"Except for one thing," Andy said. "I've been leaving the light by the front door on all night, to discourage potential vandals. Looks like it worked."

"Then why didn't you do the same at the back door?"

"The bulb was out back there. I haven't had a chance to replace it." He gave me a weak smile.

I bit my tongue. Andy needed to get his act together fast if he was going to have any success as a landlord. Maybe I should ask Pete to have a little talk with his cousin.

"And what brings you to my humble property this lovely morning?" Andy asked. "I never did give you a chance to tell me yesterday."

"I'm meeting some folks here," I checked my watch. "They should arrive shortly." I decided not to tell him who or why, at least for the moment. I always did love a surprise.

He shivered. "How about we wait for them inside? I just removed the plywood from the front door, which means it's probably not much warmer than out here, but at least there'll be no wind. And there's a space heater I can boot up for us."

"Good idea." I followed him in.

"Good morning, folks." The ServPro boss poked his head out from Ursula's first floor apartment. "Say, Andy, we'll be ready to start on the cellar soon. Do you want us to access it from the bulkhead or the inside door?"

"The bulkhead's out of commission," Andy told them. "You'll have to go down from inside. I'll get that open for you folks before I start on the front door."

"Great, Man. Thanks."

"It's a good thing they're starting work down there today," Andy said. "I don't know how much longer I could live with the smell of smoke."

I knew what he meant.

Andy was unlocking the door to the cellar when Douglas Weiss came in through what used to be the front door.

"Hey, where have you been, man?" Andy asked.

"New Hampshire," Weiss said, staring at the floor. "I took the bus up to Nashua Saturday to visit an old friend. The guy owed me money. I needed it."

"The police were here looking for you Saturday afternoon," Andy told him. "They said something about a parole violation. What's that all about?"

Weiss stood there mute.

"I didn't know what they were talking about," Andy continued. "Geez, man, why didn't you tell me you were on parole?"

"Would you have let me live here if you'd known?"

Andy thought about that for a moment. "Yeah, I would have. Absolutely."

Weiss shifted his weight from one foot to the other. "Maybe you could give me a break here. I need to clear out before the cops come back and find me. I'll just go down to the cellar to pick up some stuff I left stored down there. Stuff I'm going to need. If it wasn't damaged by the fire."

I jumped in. "It's no use, Richard. It's all over."

Richard, aka Doug, remained silent.

Andy turned to me. "What do you mean it's all over? And who are you calling Richard? What's going on here?"

I ignored Andy's questions for the moment and addressed the other man. "Yes, I know your real name. You're Richard Grant. And I know what you want in the cellar. There's no use playing dumb. The police found that suitcase the other day."

"Suitcase?" Grant asked. "What suitcase? What are you talking about?"

I bit my tongue and waited. Silence can be a wonderful tool.

Grant wouldn't look me in the eye. Playing dumb, though, was not his best trick. He stared at the floor, cracked his knuckles, chewed on his lower lip.

I watched and waited. And never said a word.

Eventually, Grant gave up. He collapsed into the wall behind him and slid to the floor. He sat there, head in hands, for a few moments, then said to Andy, "The suitcase contained the body of a baby. My son. It's been in the cellar for years. I never meant for any of this to happen. All I wanted was to give my boy a proper burial."

Andy's mouth fell open.

"I never should have buried him down there," Grant sobbed. "I shouldn't have left him like that. I realize that now. My child deserved a decent burial."

I spoke up. "And he will get one. I promise."

"Will you folks please tell me what's going on here?" Andy asked. "What are you two talking about?"

"I'll start at the beginning," I said to Andy. "The man you know as Douglas Weiss is actually named Richard Grant. He and his wife lived here years ago, with their infant son. The child died."

Grant broke in. "I didn't mean to kill him. Really I didn't. It was an accident. I loved my boy. I only wanted him to stop crying. I guess I shook him too hard. I never meant for him to die."

"I know," I said. "It was an accident."

Andy continued to stand there staring in disbelief.

"I was a real hot-head back then," Grant continued. "Had major anger issues. I couldn't help it. Just couldn't control my temper. And then my baby boy was dead."

"And your wife left," I added.

Grant's lower lip quivered. "Right. I loved Marissa. I really did. But my temper scared her. And then she rejected me. She did nothing to help me, just turned on me instead. And then she took off. She broke my heart. After I buried my son in the cellar, I had nightmares. Bad nightmares. All the time. I tried to drink them away. It didn't work. I was spiraling out of control. Lost my temper in a bar one night. Got into a fight. I didn't know my own strength. The guy died. I got locked away. For a long time." He put his head in his hands and wept.

Andy and I waited silently, allowing Grant time to pull himself together.

Finally, he resumed his story. "I got help while I was in prison. Anger management, they called it. They gave me some meds as well. It took years, but it finally helped. When I got paroled, my first thought was to come back here and do the right thing for my son. He deserved it. So I became Douglas Weiss, moved in and waited for the opportunity to retrieve my son's body and lay it in a decent grave."

"And then it all went wrong," I said.

"That was an accident too." His voice shook. "That dude with the sword in the weird white clothes. The fire. I never meant for any of that to happen."

"I know you didn't," I said. "And the police know it as well."

Grant's eyes suddenly widened as he stared straight ahead. Marissa stood there in the hallway, just inside the space where the door belonged. Her husband Chet, in his police uniform, was by her side. Grant leapt to his feet and shouted. "What the Hell are you doing here? And why did you bring the cops with you?"

Marissa remained in the hallway, remarkably calm. "Chet isn't here as a cop, Richard. He's here as my husband."

"Husband? What the Hell are you talking about? I'm your husband."

"Sorry, Richard. That marriage was annulled years ago. You were notified. I mailed you the paperwork here myself."

He shook his head. "Trouble is I wasn't here. Must've been in prison by then." He choked back a sob. "Then why are you here?"

"For the same reason you are. To bury our son."

Grant turned to where Andy and I were standing. "It's all her fault, you know. She never should have left the baby with me. I couldn't care for him. I wasn't any good at it. She knew that. It was all her fault Timmy died."

The man we'd been speaking with just minutes earlier was gone. An angry, agitated person had taken his place. Marissa sure wasn't kidding when she told me of his violent mood swings. "Please calm down, Richard," I said to him.

"The Hell I will!" He was shouting now. "That bitch ruined my life. She deserves to die. And so do you for bringing her here."

"Doug," Andy said, "or Richard, please listen to me. We can make this right."

"I'm not listening to nobody," Richard shouted. He grabbed me from behind and pulled me close to him with one arm. With his other arm, he reached into Andy's tool belt and pulled out a knife.

Holding the knife to my throat, he shouted, "I'm not going back to prison. I can't. I did my time. I'm going to walk out of here now. And nobody's coming after me. Or this lovely lady dies."

With my heart pounding in my chest, I held my breath and tried to pretend I wasn't scared witless.

"Please. Let her go," Andy said.

"Can't do that," Richard said. "Now back off, all of you." He glared at Marissa's husband. "And don't even think about pulling out your gun. Or she dies."

CHAPTER 36

ndy, Marissa and her husband stood in the hallway looking every bit as helpless and horrified as I felt. The Servpro boss emerged from Ursula's apartment. He took one look at the scene before him and ducked back inside.

Then Marissa found her voice. She spoke softly and slowly, with enough warmth to thaw the coldest of hearts. "Richard, please, listen to me. I know it was an accident. Everybody knows that. Nobody is blaming you for what happened. You have to believe me."

"About Timmy, sure. I get that now. But what about that other guy?"

"You mean on New Year's Day?" I asked.

"Right. The dude with the sword."

"He was a fencer," I said. "He had a name. Howie Zupkoff."

"Yeah, whatever." Grant stopped shouting. He seemed calmer now, but he maintained an iron grip on me, and kept the knife at my throat. "You've got to listen to me. Believe me. I didn't mean to do it. It was his fault." Grant closed his eyes and took a deep breath. We waited silently for him to continue.

"The guy got what was coming to him. He had no business sneaking up on me like that. I didn't even know he was there until I hit him with the pick mattock. And I saw him lying there bleeding. It was an accident."

I needed to keep Grant talking. Detective Donnelly was on his way. I only hoped he'd arrive in time to save me.

"We know that now," I said. "I know it. The police know it. Accidents happen." I knew how lame and ludicrous that sounded, but I was becoming desperate. I'd say pretty much anything to get this guy to put the knife away and let me go.

A loud noise from the front porch interrupted my terror. Someone was knocking on the plywood and shouting, "Hello? Anybody home?"

Andy, Marissa, Chet and I all turned to Grant.

"Who's there?" Grant shouted. "What do you want?"

"I've got a delivery for you. Two doors and a window."

Grant looked at Andy. "You expecting something?"

Andy nodded. "Two doors and a window. Ordered them this morning."

Grant grunted. "Yeah. Right."

"Can you leave everything out behind the house?" Andy called to the delivery man.

"Sorry," was the response. "No can do. You gotta sign for them."

Andy gave Grant a "what can I do?" look.

Grant knit his brows. "O.K. Go. But don't try anything funny. And get rid of him fast. Or I use this knife on her." He pushed me forward to make room for Andy to squeeze past him and to the rear door.

While Grant was watching Andy leave, I mouthed to Marissa and her husband, "Go. Run. Now." I jutted my chin to indicate the front entrance.

They bolted.

Now it was just me and Richard Grant. And the knife at my throat.

As much as I hated to beg and plead and sound needy, that was rapidly becoming my only, my final, recourse. I girded my loins and modulated my voice. "Listen, Richard, I know you don't want to hurt me. Not really. You know it too. We can explain what happened to the police. They'll understand."

"Who's going to believe an ex-con like me?"

"I believe you." I told him.

"And so do I." A voice that sounded like Pete's came through the back door.

Grant started at the sound of Pete's voice. "And who the Hell are you?"

"I'm the guy who's trying to stop you from cutting the throat of the woman I love."

That did me in. I let out a loud sob.

Grant loosened his grip ever so slightly. "You mean this lady?"

"Yes I do," Pete said. "Please, just listen to me. You've got no way out of this. You can't run. The police have the house surrounded."

That news gave me a glimmer of hope.

"Tell them to go away," Grant shouted as he tightened his grip on me.

"I can't do that," Pete said. "Please, Mr. Grant, just put down the knife. Let Amy go. Let me find somebody to help you."

Grant became deadly still and quiet, apparently mulling this over. "Sorry, dude. I wish I could. But I don't know you. Don't know if I can trust you. Right now this lady here is the only sure way I can get out of here alive. And you know that as well as I do."

I waited to hear Pete's response to this ultimatum. What I heard instead was a loud noise, like the report of a gun being fired at close range. I smelled the sulfur. Grant's body lurched forward into me, I felt a sticky wetness on my right shoulder and my back. Then I closed my eyes and felt nothing as Grant and I collapsed to the floor.

CHAPTER 37

When I came to, Pete was kneeling over me with tears running down his cheeks. "It's all right, Ames," he said. "You're going to be fine."

"I guess that means I'm not dead," I replied.

He shook his head. "Actually, you're not even injured."

I found that hard to believe. "Then why am I covered with blood?"

Pete smiled and glanced over to his left. "That's not your blood. It's Richard Grant's." I followed his eyes to find a bloody, agitated Richard Grant lying face-down on the floor with Andy and the ServPro men doing their best to keep him subdued while Marissa's husband handcuffed him. Turning to Pete, I said, "Surrounded by the police, huh? Looks more like surrounded by a lawyer, a landlord, a ServPro crew and an out-of-town cop." Not to mention a fellow who must be the delivery man bringing up the rear and staring at us all with his mouth open and his eyes wide.

Pete grinned. "And yet, we got the job done."

I gave this some thought. "My questions is: how did I not get injured? It appears that Grant was shot at close range. Why didn't the bullet pass through him and into me?"

"That's easy," Marissa's policeman husband replied. "First of all, I'm a pretty good shot. And I crouched, so I'd be shooting up at Grant. Add to that the fact that you're shorter than the average person, and there you go. The bullet went through Grant's upper arm, disabling it, then it kept right on going into the wall."

And that saved my life, thanks be to God. "What happens now?" I asked.

"The police are on their way," Pete said, "as well as an ambulance for our friend here."

Grant chose that moment to resume his tirade. "No!" he howled. "No police. I can't go back to prison. Please. Don't let them take me. Don't let them send me away again." He was on the verge of hysterics. Only his weakened condition made it possible for Andy and the ServPro gang to hold him down.

"You're going to the hospital," Pete said to him. "You need medical attention. You've lost a lot of blood."

Pete's words were drowned out by a ruckus in the street out front. I turned my head to see the arrival of Detective Donnelly, two uniformed policemen and two EMTs with a gurney.

Donnelly spoke first. "Howdy folks. Sure looks like I missed all the fun here. And Mr. Grant, we've been looking for you."

Grant glared up at Donnelly and spat.

Donnelly signaled to the EMTs. "Go ahead, guys. Have at him."

The EMTs examined Grant quickly and efficiently and applied a tourniquet to his arm to stop the bleeding.

Donnelly watched as they worked. "How bad is it?"

One of the EMTs looked up at Donnelly. "It's nowhere near as bad as it looks. The bullet passed through his upper arm, hitting the brachial artery along the way. That's why there's so much blood."

"Is he in a lot of pain?" Donnelly asked.

The EMT shook his head. "Actually, very little at the moment. Adrenalin is keeping it at bay for now."

207

"Does that mean you're not in a hurry here?"

"Correct."

Donnelly smiled. "Excellent. Since he's not critical, I'd like to ask him a few questions before you take him away." He looked down at Grant. "Tell me, where have you been keeping yourself?"

"Nowhere. Not that it's any of your damn business. I've got rights, you know."

Donnelly shook his head. "I think not. We came by here Saturday, hoping to speak with you about the fire. We also went to Newton. You were nowhere to be found."

Richard Grant, suddenly calm again, heaved a mighty sigh and frowned. "You have me at a disadvantage. I guess there's no point arguing with you at the moment, never mind trying to get away."

Donnelly rolled his eyes. "Definitely not on my watch. And now we have a lot more to talk about than just the fire. We've got serious questions about more than one deceased individual."

"No way," Grant said, suddenly agitated again. "You can't pin any of that on me. They told me you knew it was an accident. About the baby. About the guy with the sword. Everything. You can't arrest me for an accident."

"The fact that it was an accident makes it manslaughter, not murder. That is still a chargeable offense." Donnelly replied. "And we've got you on a few other charges as well."

"Like what?" Grant spat. "I didn't do nothing else. What are you talking about?"

"What about Beatrice Vaughn? Did you attack her?"

"Huh? Who? Do you mean that old lady?"

"Indeed I do. A sweet, innocent old lady."

"She wasn't innocent. She was dangerous. I didn't want to hurt her. But she recognized me. From years ago. She could've ruined everything. I couldn't take the chance." He screwed up his face. "You're not gonna tell me she's dead, are you?"

"Lucky for you, she is going to make it. But we will be charging you with assault. And we've also got you on breaking and entering," Donnelly said.

Grant stared at the bloody floor and said nothing.

"Then there's the matter of parole violation," Donnelly continued. "I spoke with your parole officer this morning. He hasn't heard from you in months."

"You can't send me back to that joint," Grant said. "No way. I can't do it. I can't hack it. I did my time." He let out a sob so mighty that his entire bloody body shook.

"A good lawyer may be able to help you with that," Pete spoke up.

Everybody turned to Pete.

"What the hell are you talking about?" Grant asked. "Can't afford no lawyer,"

"You won't have to," Pete told him.

Andy stared at Pete open-mouthed. "Hold on there, Pete. You're not offering to defend this guy, are you?"

"Hell no. He just threatened to kill the love of my life. I can't get past that. The court will appoint a lawyer, Mr. Grant, at no cost to you."

"Will he get me off?" Grant asked.

"Under the current circumstances, probably not. I can, however, assure you that whoever it is will do his utmost to get you the best possible deal," Pete said.

Grant stared at Pete, but said nothing.

"OK, fellas," Donnelly said to the EMTs. "You can take him away now."

We all watched in silence as the gurney bearing Richard Grant was moved out of the house and into the ambulance.

"As for the rest of you," Donnelly said, "We're going to need statements." He turned to one of the uniformed officers with him. "Mulcahey, you take our friends from ServPro and this delivery guy.

I'm sure they're all itching to get back to work. As for the rest of you, I'm afraid I have to ask you to come down to the station with me. I'll see if I can arrange for the coroner to join us there as well."

"Does that mean I'll be able to bury my baby soon?" Marissa asked him.

Donnelly gave her a sad smile. "I'll see what I can do."

CHAPTER 38

The remainder of the day consisted of meetings with the police and the coroner, filling out paperwork, and answering endless questions. Both Detective Donnelly and Ted Rosen, the medical examiner, dealt with Marissa and her husband first so they could drive back to Great Barrington in time for Chet to get to work. A thoughtful gesture.

As for me, I felt more like a suspect than a witness. Donnelly was nice about it, just doing his job, he said. I understood that, even though I didn't like it.

Pete stayed with me through the whole ordeal, then drove me home. He left for a while, then returned with Thai take-out, the ultimate urban comfort food, and a bottle of some lovely single-malt scotch.

"I was proud of you today," he said as he served the food. "You handled yourself so well. Every bit your usual brave self."

I took a long swig of scotch. "Brave nothing," I said. "I was scared to death. Just too damn stubborn to admit it."

He laughed.

"You were pretty impressive yourself," I told him. "The way you guys took Grant down was like something right out of a movie." I lifted my glass. "Here's to you, my love."

211

Pete laughed again. "I'm not sure I should admit this to you, but that part was actually kind of fun."

"For you, perhaps. Not so for me." I grinned at him, then asked, "Do you think a court-appointed attorney will be able to get Grant off?"

He shook his head. "Not even close. But I'm certain he can get a fair deal."

Leave it to Pete to think of that. "Any idea how Grant is doing?"

"Yes. While you folks were dealing with the medical examiner, Detective Donnelly caught me up on Grant's situation. He's heavily sedated at the moment and will spend the night in the hospital. Once he's released, he'll be arraigned and remanded to the Suffolk County House of Corrections pending trial."

"I'm guessing he'll plead some sort of an insanity defense." From what I had seen, that made sense.

Pete frowned. "It would be better for him if he didn't."

I gave him what I felt was an incredulous look. "Explain that, if you please."

"With pleasure. While there are several charges against Grant, most of what Donnelly mentioned are minor offenses, such as breaking and entering or violating parole. Everybody agreed that both deaths, the baby's and Howie Zupkoff's, were involuntary manslaughter."

"What about Beatrice's mugging? Don't forget that."

"Right, but that was his first offense of that kind."

"All of which adds up to what? Was the man sane when he did all these things?"

"That's not the major concern here," Pete explained. "He already did hard time. And when he got out, he was actually trying to make things right, to bury his child. That has to count for something."

I wasn't so sure about that. Apparently I was nowhere near as charitable as Pete. "Tell me how this all works."

"If Grant pleads insanity, he'll be sent to the Bridgewater Correctional Facility. Folks who are placed there often end up staying for life. It's just the way the system works. If sanity is not an issue, and Grant pleads guilty, it could help him get a lighter sentence, and in a minimum security prison, like Plymouth. That way, the guy would have an easier time during his incarceration, as well as a decent chance of serving less time. Maybe a little more anger management therapy is all he really needs. You never know."

"Like I said, you're a nice guy. What about Charlie Florescu? Any news on him?"

"He is in major big-time trouble. That guy is one bad dude. I hope he gets exactly what he deserves."

"Amen to that."

We snuggled on the couch after we ate. I clung to Pete like my life depended on it, as it recently had.

I may have overdone the scotch a bit, because the next thing I knew it was morning and the two of us were still on the couch, tangled under an afghan and stiff and achy. And oh-so-very happy to be there. My near-death experience had left me feeling lucky in a lot of ways.

Pete left to check in with his office. I knew I should do the same, but wasn't quite ready to act on that thought. The phone rang when I was half-way through my second cup of coffee.

Detective Donnelly.

"Good morning, Detective."

"Right back at you." He hesitated, then added, "I just wanted to thank you for your help with our friend Richard Grant yesterday. And to congratulate you on the way you handled things. You did yourself proud."

"Thanks. It means a lot to hear you say that. Where do things stand as of this morning? Pete filled me in on Grant's situation once he's out of the hospital."

"He's being released sometime this morning and taken into custody. The system, such as it is, will take it from there."

"And what about the baby's remains?"

"Being transferred even as we speak. The mother is working with a funeral home out her way on the final arrangements."

"That's good news." I'd follow up on that later with Marissa. I wanted to be there for her.

I rang off with Donnelly and prepared to go to the office. I was eager to handle the final paperwork and put Andy's claim to rest.

CHAPTER 39

Two days later, we returned to the Berkshires for Timmy Grant's funeral. Mrs. Czwakiel and Ursula Fagan came as well, though they rode with Andy. The back seat of my Mustang convertible was far too small, too much of a challenge for them and Pete's car was in the shop for some minor issue.

The drive seemed somehow longer today than it had last Saturday. The traffic wasn't the problem. That moved fine. The issue was more the sad event which awaited us in the Berkshires.

Marissa had opted for a full funeral mass at St. Joseph's Church in Stockbridge. She said it would bring her true closure. I applauded her decision, though I knew the day would be difficult for her.

St. Joseph's was a pretty little stone church. The parking lot held only two other cars, Andy's Toyota and a blue SUV I recognized as belonging to Marissa and Chet. As we pulled in, I asked Pete, "Have you ever been to this church?"

He shook his head. "No. Why do you ask?"

"Because that means you get to make three wishes," I explained. "You always do when you enter a new church."

"This church doesn't look so new," he grinned.

"You know what I mean. New as in you haven't been there before."

He rolled his eyes. "I'm guessing your mother told you about these wishes."

"She did. And my mother wouldn't lie to me."

"Well then, I guess I should wish that we don't get caught when we go to bury St. Joseph in that lawyer's front yard in Walpole."

I sighed loudly as we headed into the church. It was cool inside, and dimly lit. A tiny coffin stood in front of the altar. It was enough to break my heart.

Marissa and her family were in the first row. Her two sons appeared to be in their tweens. They also seemed to be more than a little uncomfortable in their suits and ties. Poor kids. This had to be hard for them. Marissa glanced back and acknowledged our presence with a solemn nod. Then she rested her head on her husband's shoulder, a weary look on her face.

Andy, Ursula and Mrs. Czwakiel occupied the pew behind the Arnolds. Pete and I settled into the third pew as the funeral mass began. The priest identified himself as Father Williams. I had heard that name before. He was the priest who helped Marissa obtain an annulment of her marriage to Richard Grant.

The service was less grim than I had feared, concentrating on closure, and little Timmy finally resting in peace. The soloist did herself proud. Her selection of music was uplifting rather than morbidly sad. Nevertheless, Marissa wiped her eyes more than once. I did as well. And then it was over. Pete and I joined the solemn procession behind that tiny coffin and headed to the door of the church.

There was no service at the cemetery. The ground was too frozen and snow-covered for an actual burial. That would have to wait until spring. One more ordeal for Marissa to endure.

Outside the church, Marissa and Chet introduced their sons to us. Billy, age 10 and Dave age 12. Good-looking boys. They both resembled their father. Neither had much to say to us. That was actually all right with me. I never knew what to say to boys that age. Pete asked them what sports they played and got them chatting about baseball.

Chet invited us all to join them for lunch at a nearby restaurant. Michael's was a short drive from the church. It was casual and kid friendly, serving what they referred to as American food.

We settled in at a long table in the rear of the room. Pete, Andy, Chet and the two boys took up one end of the table. Father Williams, Ursula and Mrs. Czwakiel joined Marissa and me at the other end. Marissa made an obvious point of sitting next to me.

I searched for something appropriate to say which would help dispel the gloom which had settled over us.

Father Williams saved me the trouble. He lifted his water glass and said, "Here's to you, Timmy. Home at last. Let us give thanks for the miracle that brought him back to us."

"Yes," Marissa said, turning to me. "Thank you for finding my baby."

"And for bringing peace to my wife," her husband added.

"And thank you for saving my life," I said to Chet. "If you weren't such a crack shot, I wouldn't be here today."

Chet blushed.

The younger son, Billy, spoke up. "And thank you Mom and Dad for saying that Dave and I can have brownie sundaes for dessert." That brought on a laugh and relieved the tension.

Ursula spoke up. "As sad as this occasion is, I am still happy to see you again, Marissa. I enjoyed our friendship back in Dorchester. And our walks around the neighborhood."

Marissa seconded that thought.

"Speaking of neighbors," Ursula said as she turned to Mrs. Czwakiel, "I can't believe you didn't recognize Richard Grant when he returned to Chadwick Street as Douglas Weiss."

Mrs. Czwakiel sighed. "I know. As I think about it now, he really hadn't changed all that much. Older and hairier, but that's all."

Ursula laughed. "Then apparently your eyesight has changed, or your memory. Perhaps both."

"What can I say?" Mrs. Czwakiel replied. "Old age is tough, definitely not for the faint of heart. Beatrice recognized the man and I doubted her word. I must apologize to her for that."

"Speaking of Beatrice," I joined in, "is there any news on her condition?"

"I checked with the hospital this morning," Andy said.

I smiled at Pete. "Andy is such a nice guy."

"It runs in the family," Pete replied, then turned to Andy and said, "And …?"

"And she's doing much better. They expect to release her tomorrow or the next day."

"That's good news," Mrs. Czwakiel said. "When I visited her on Monday, she was still in pretty bad shape. That's where I was when all the hullabaloo was happening on Chadwick Street. It seems that I missed quite a show."

Marissa's husband spoke up. "I'm still not quite clear on the sequence of events that led to finding the baby."

"That's understandable," I told him. "There were some strange twists and turns along the way."

"Right," Andy said. "If Howie Zupkoff wasn't looking to score some drugs, he never would have been in the cellar to begin with. If there hadn't been a fire, his body wouldn't have been found so soon. And if the police hadn't been in the cellar investigating his death, they never would have found the baby's grave at that time. It could have remained there forever."

"And the fire never would have happened if Ellen hadn't fought with Charlie Florescu" I added, "and gone down to the cellar to console herself with marijuana."

"And around and around it goes," Pete said. "An odd combination of random events resulting in something good."

I poked him in the ribs. "We'll discuss this in detail later. Don't forget our bet."

When the guys at the other end of the table began talking about the Red Sox. and Father Williams, Ursula and Mrs. Czwakiel were deep in conversation about their favorite daytime TV shows, Marissa patted my arm to get my attention. "You seem to have recovered quite well from your ordeal the other day. That had to be so frightening for you."

"It was. But I'm tougher than I look."

"Apparently so." She frowned deeply. "And I'm so sorry you had to witness one of Richard's violent rages. I guess you can understand now why I was so frightened of him."

"That's for sure," I said, shuddering at the memory of his assault on me.

Marissa sighed. "It's amazing to think that I loved him once. As I told you, he could be charming at times. I only hope he gets the help he needs now. Perhaps prison will do him some good. But if it doesn't, I hope they keep him there for a very long time."

The luncheon ended on a positive note. Marissa appeared more relaxed. She smiled some, listened to Mrs. Czwakiel gossip about the neighbors and commiserated with Ursula about her failing health. They made plans to stay in touch, perhaps even get together from time to time.

When Pete and I said our good-byes, Marissa said to me, "I don't know how to thank you for everything you've done. And then for your company to cover the cost of the funeral was so very generous." She gave me a hug.

I had no idea what she meant but simply returned the hug and said, "You're welcome." I couldn't wait to speak with Peggy and get the scoop on that. I pulled out my phone to call her as Pete entered the on-ramp to the Mass Pike.

"I've got to ask you something," Pete said.

"What's that?"

"Why do you spend so much time speaking on the phone? Why not just text people?"

"Two reasons. First, I'm all thumbs when it comes to texting, if you know what I mean. Guess I just lack the appropriate manual dexterity."

"You could learn, you know. Practicing making perfect and whatnot."

"I don't really want to," I told him. "I prefer to hear a human voice. You can learn a lot from the way things are said. Tone of voice, for instance, can be very telling. You miss that in a text. Sometimes it matters. Face to face is better still. And when I'm driving, it's safer to talk than to text. Talk hands-free, of course."

"Now that I think about it, I believe you are right about that."

"As I often am," I said as I punched in Peggy's number. "What's going on?" I asked as soon as I heard her voice.

"And hello to you too," she replied. "Which goings-on are in question?"

"The baby's funeral. Marissa was grateful that NEC&I footed the bill for it."

"Right."

"What do you mean 'Right?' I'm happy that we paid for it, but I don't understand exactly how that came about."

Peggy laughed. "Would you believe that George arranged it?"

"George?"

"Yes. He said it could be covered under the Collateral Damage Clause."

"There is no Collateral Damage Clause in the policy."

"I know that," Peggy laughed again, "though I let George think I believed him. And he specifically told me not to tell you."

That made me smile. "So he was worried that somebody might catch him doing something nice."

"So it seems," Peggy said.

"Well, wonders never cease," I replied. "Let's not let him know we're on to him." I disconnected the call and said to Pete, "OK, Buddy. Now about that bet we made ..."

CHAPTER 40

Pete and I were at a quiet corner table at Gaslight, a genuine French Brasserie in Boston, one of my all-time favorite restaurants. It had fabulous ambience, amazing food and a four-star rating. That was fine with me. I was happy to forgo the fifth star included in our bet to be in the best bistro this side of Paris.

The waiter uncorked a bottle of Vouvray, then took our hors d'oeuvres order – escargots to share and a charcuterie and cheese board. We didn't order our entrées yet. Pete had settled on the roast duck, but I was still struggling between the clams with pernod and the lemon sole. A touch decision.

Pete filled me in on the latest news while I weighed my options. "I spoke with Andy today. He said his claim check from NEC&I was already in the bank and he was ready to roll with the work on the house."

"I'm pleased we were able to pay him so quickly," I said. "And now that ServPro has finished their clean-up, Andy's in pretty good shape as far as repairs go. He has already replaced the busted doors and windows. The remaining damage is largely contained to the floors and walls of the first floor apartment on the left."

Pete pursed his lips. "True. But I'm trying to convince him to do as many additional updates as he can manage. At least repaint the walls and clean up the floors in the other five units. And all the kitchens and bathrooms could use a major overhaul while he's at it."

"Kitchens and bathrooms are expensive. Can he afford that?"

Pete squirmed. "I offered him a small loan to cover that. It just makes sense to do it all at once. That'll make the place rentable sooner. And also command a higher rent."

"You are a good guy, Pete Devereaux."

"I try." He blushed.

Our hors d'oeuvres arrived. We ordered entrees – I finally decided on the sole – then ordered a second bottle of Vouvray and dug into the escargots.

Between bites, I said to Pete, "I'm so relieved that Andy is in the clear. I didn't enjoy considering him as a suspect."

Pete nodded. "That's for sure." He cut himself a chunk of Brie, then added, "That was a big worry for a while there. I'd rather have him be a big cry baby any day. Andy also said he heard from Freddy. The McGill fencing team has established a fund in Howie's honor. The Howard Zupkoff Memorial Scholarship. They've already collected over $100,000."

"What a wonderful way to honor Howie, although I think they probably did it out of guilt."

"What do you mean?"

"The rest of the team didn't care much for Howie. They weren't particularly nice to him. And then he was dead. Anyway, I'm sure his family is pleased." I paused for a moment to pull my thoughts together. "Now, about that bet we made … "

"Are you still going to try to convince me there's no such thing as coincidence? That things happened as they were destined to?" He laughed.

"You bet I am. It was all connected. It had to be."

"Go on."

"It's like we discussed after the funeral the other day. All the 'but fors.' What you insist on viewing as random events were actually tied together by cause and effect. One thing led to another until they all came together."

"Huh? Are you trying to tell me it was all part of some cosmic plan?"

"It was certainly no coincidence that Richard Grant moved back into the house on Chadwick Street."

"What about Howie Zupkoff?" Pete asked.

"He was in that cellar for a reason."

Pete shook his head. "Yeah. To buy drugs, not to get killed. Or was that supposed to happen?"

I had to think about that. Finally, I replied, "Perhaps if he had lived he would have become a serial killer, or something equally dreadful." I washed that thought down with some Vouvray.

"Give me a break." Pete responded. "That's just nuts. And what about Grant returning to the house the very morning Marissa was coming there?"

I had him there. "I fully expected that to happen. He had unfinished business in the cellar. Had no idea the baby's body had been found."

Pete put down his fork and looked at me. "What about your own near-death experience? Was that supposed to happen as well?"

I had no good answer for that. "That was just an unfortunate side effect. I certainly wasn't supposed to die. Not yet. Not for a long time. I'm going to stick around for years to keep an eye on you. And to fill your life with joy – or some such horse puckey."

"Lucky me," he said. "But you still haven't convinced me it's all not simple coincidence."

I thought for a moment. "Think of it as convergence."

"I'm listening."

I struggled to explain. "Look at it this way. We've got two different threads of events going on. There's Richard Grant burying the baby years ago, then returning to dig the poor thing up and accidentally killing Howie in the process."

"I'm with you so far."

"Then there's the Charlie Florescu thread. Baiting Howie, then fighting with Ellen. Which resulted in her going down to the cellar, discovering Howie's body and accidentally causing the fire."

"You just mentioned two unrelated series of accidents. Where's the convergence?" Pete shook his head.

"It's in the coming together of the two threads. And when these threads converged, all Hell broke loose. The combination of Grant's actions and Florescu's came together in the cellar, resulting in Howie's death, the fire and Timmy's body being found then laid to rest."

Pete sighed and rolled his eyes. "You mean like it was supposed to happen that way? So the baby would be found? Give me a break here, Ames."

I took his hand. "My poor prosaic Pete. Is there no poetry in your soul? No sense of wonder?"

"Sure. Sometimes I wonder what actually goes on in that head of yours," he began, then caught himself and added, "Most of all I wonder how I got lucky enough to have you in my life."

"Good save, Buddy."

"So what do you think?" he asked. "Who won the bet?"

I laughed. "I think we better split the check."

ABOUT THE AuTHOR

Like her heroine Amy Lynch, P.K. (Paula) Norton spent her career in the insurance industry. When she and her late husband Jack traveled throughout the U.S. and abroad, they entertained themselves by sitting in restaurants discussing interesting ways to kill people. As they plotted all manner of mysterious deaths and mayhem, the world of Amy Lynch was born. Paula's passions also become an integral part of her series—interests such as archeology (Paula has lived in Paris and once worked at the archaeological dig described in Dead Drop), spies (Paula was a card carrying member of The Association of Former Intelligence Officers), Paris, Key West and fencing. Direct Elimination is the fourth book of the Amy Lynch Investigations. Two more stories are currently in the works."

When she is not plotting and writing, Paula is, well, plotting and writing. She is a member of Sisters in Crime, the Cape Cod Writers' Association and the Rhode Island Authors Association.

Paula resides in Easton, MA.